HOR

Volume 2
(Cryptids)

Edited by Colin C. Martin

HORRORific Tales   (Cryptids)

HORRORific Tales Volume 2 (Cryptids)

Paperback Edition ISBN 978-1-0684637-0-9

Published by HORRORific Productions Ltd
61 Bridge Street, Kington, Herefordshire,
HR5 3DJ, England, United Kingdom

HORRORific Publishing, The HORRORific Podcast and their logos are trademarks of HORRORific Productions Ltd.

A Deep Dark Sorrow @Del Gibson 2025
A Jersey Devil of a Time @Anthony M Caro 2025
Elijah's Shadow @Justine Johnston Hemmestad 2025
His Grandmother's Eyes @Bruce Buchanan 2025
Husker @Lee Swift 2025
La LeChuza @Eugene McLean 2025
Where Lava Flows @Demi Michelle Schwartz 2025
The Shadow off Slieveanorra @Colin C Martin 2025
Eyja Beinannar The Island of the Bones @Eli Beals 2025
Salivating, Drooling Evil @Arthur L 2025

The Devil's Fingerprints @Gary Batchelor 2025

The authors assert the moral right to be identified as the author of their work

No part of this publication may be reproduced, stored in a retrieval system or transmitted, in any form or by any means without the prior written permission of the publisher. Nor may it be otherwise circulated in any form of binding or cover other than in which it is published and without a similar condition being imposed on the subsequent purchaser.

A CIP catalogue number for this title is available from the British Library

HORRORific Tales   (Cryptids)

This book is dedicated to independent creators trying to make their way in the world. By honing your craft and not taking the easy payout from the bland, sterile corporations you inspire us, spark our imaginations and make us believe that anything is possible. Keep striving on your journey, stay true to yourself and may every success that you deserve arrive at your door.

Special thanks to Cameron, Chris, Del, Stephen and FL_3 for being my co-hosts, inner circle and close support as I've went on this creative journey. Here's to the beginning of something truly HORRORific!

Thank you also to the myriads of independent creators who have interacted with our podcast and publisher over the years. You have helped to inspire me to keep going and to put something out into the world.

HORRORific Tales   (Cryptids)

Are they an undiscovered species or just pseudoscience? We may never truly reveal the truth behind these creatures of folklore and mystery. Cryptids have been lurking in the shadows since before the existence of humanity. Not many people survive encounters with these beings. Those that do are changed forever!

Contents

Introduction by Colin C. Martin	8
A Deep Sorrow by Del Gibson	13
A Jersey Devil of a Time by Anthony M Caro	55
Elijah's Shadow by Justine Johnson Hemmestad	73
His Grandmother's Eyes by Bruce Buchanan	89
Husker by Lee Swift	123
La Lechuza by Eugene McLean	157
Where Lava Flows by Demi Michelle Schwartz	179
The Shadow of Slieveanorra by Colin C Martin	205
Eyja Beinannar - The Island Of the Bones by Eli Beals	225
Salivating, Drooling Evil by Arthur L	243
The Devil's Fingerprints by Gary Batchelor	263
The Cryptid Catalogue	293

HORRORific Tales   (Cryptids)

Introduction

Well folks! Here we are again. I am absolutely amazed at the pace that this series is coming along, from the initial concept in late 2024 to this second publication which you are enjoying now. The amount of goodwill and support that came with the advent of Volume One which has followed through to this publication has been amazing. Thank you for coming on board, whether as a reader or as a contributor. I really appreciate you.

With this fantastic feeling of accomplishment also comes a sense of responsibility. I don't forget for one minute the talented individuals who have entrusted their stories to me and to this series. It takes a lot to pour your thoughts and feelings into a piece of work and more importantly hand that over to someone else. I'll always be honoured by the trust that has been placed in me.

My first encounter with Cryptids was the tale of the Loch Ness Monster. The idea of something huge and ancient living amongst us was thrilling. I remember the documentaries on TV trying to uncover the mystery of this beast. The use of modern technology and investigative techniques only generated more questions than answers. This helped to cement the idea that there were still wonders in the world that we could not comprehend.

An aspect of the Internet that I really love is that we now have access to similar stories across the world and their tellers. We don't have to wait until a movie gets made to learn about the various wonders of each land. We can look into these things now without having our hands held by mainstream entertainment companies. I've even been surprised by the number of local legends and stories that are out there that are simply not told anymore.

One thing that I hope to achieve with this series is not just to provide some entertainment but to hopefully reignite your interest in local folklore, wherever your locale may happen to be. Storytelling is an essential part of the human condition. It elevates us to being more than mere drones destined to a life of drudgery and mediocrity. It reminds us that there are still unknowns out there. It sparks our imagination and inspires us to be greater. We have heroes to root for and villains to scorn. Sometimes the sides aren't so clear, and we are left to ponder where our individual moral compasses point to.

HORRORific Tales   (Cryptids)

Thank you for picking up this collection of tales. I look forward to you experiencing these great stories that follow. That just leaves me to say. Until next time my friends. Remember to Keep it creepy, keep it HORRORific!

Yours in appreciation.

Colin C Martin

The HORRORific Podcast is available on numerous platforms. Find us where you usually get your podcasts here:

HORRORific Tales (Cryptids)

The HORROFfic Podcast is available on numerous platforms. Find us where you usually get your podcasts from.

A Deep Dark Sorrow

by
Del Gibson

HORRORific Tales   (Cryptids)

I'm floating in the dark abyss of a nightmare with my twin brother Aiden and we are at Wellington Zoo. Suddenly, he's yelling and running away from me and I can't catch up with him. I look back over my shoulder and a huge black snake is chasing us. Then, Aiden dives into Wellington harbour to escape it but it follows him into the water and I can't stop screaming…

The Exorcist theme song rips me from my nightmare and I know it's Dex my partner on the force calling me.

"Do you know it's 3am? Jerk!" I say, my voice sounding like there's a frog wedged in my throat.

"Jules, get your ass in here now; we've found a body in the harbour," Dex says.

"Shit! Don't go anywhere without me. Promise me. It could be one of the missing boys."

"Let's not get ahead of ourselves, we won't know for sure until we get out there," he says.

I switch to speaker phone as I rapidly dress in yesterday's clothes.

Then I head into the kitchen.

"Tell me more," I yell across the room as I make

a quick coffee in my travel mug for the twenty-minute drive into the police station.

"A fishing crew heading in from the Cook Strait found the body floating in the harbour. That's all I know. The Maritime Unit are preparing now; they'll be heading out at sunrise. I'll see you soon."

He hangs up. I start trembling as a cold chill feathers down my back, and goose pimples raise the hairs upon my skin.

It's still dark when I get outside; the sun has yet to spread its morning glory. I turn the heater on when I climb inside my Nissan SUV. On the stereo, *Queen* is singing about being a champion. I get stuck in traffic along the motorway on my way into the city. When the news comes on there is no mention about the body in the water. At least those journo leaches and the morons who eavesdrop on police scanners must still be in a deep slumber. That's good news for once.

I'm about to get out of my car when a knock on the window half scares me to death.

It's Dex.

"Fuck, dude! I could have shot your head off. Lucky for you I left my Glock at home. Actually. That's not such a bad idea," my chuckle sounds slightly withered to my ears.

"We're taking your car. They are loading the police boat, take us there," Dex commands.

"Yes sir, on the double." I do a two-finger salute in a fuck you gesture. "So, what's got your nickers in a twist? No, let me guess. Liz finally came to her senses and eloped with the gardener?" I crack myself up, it helps to tame my anxiety.

"What. No good morning, how the hell are you, no thank you fucking much for waking me up at the witching hour. Some men!" I comment, knowing full well I can feel adrenalin pumping through me, it's so fast I can feel my heart beating like a drum through my chest.

A golden pre-dawn glow glistens upon the water as we speed our way across the harbour. In the corner of my eye I see something come up through the waves, then it dives down so fast that I nearly miss it. It must be an Orca; we get those in the harbour a lot. As we pull in alongside the fishing vessel, I jump onto it and I land so hard that my teeth rattle. Dex is yelling at me, though I can't hear a word he's saying. I stoop down on my knees beside the body; the deck is wet, it soaks through my pants and the stench of fish is so nauseating that I have to try hard to stop myself from throwing up. The body's wrists and ankles are bound with what looks like duct tape, and he's too bloated to be able to visually identify him in this condition. I notice something unusual when I look closer.

"Are those bite marks?" I ask Dex when he finally reaches me.

"You're right. It looks like he's been partially eaten by a Whale or a Shark. Sharks aren't common in the harbour, perhaps it happened in the straits? Loads of Sharks travel through there. Plus, I'm pretty sure Whales don't eat people," he replies, looking as puzzled as me.

"See. I told you so! I bet it's one of the boys," I mutter.

"Yes, it could be. I'll get Arnie to go over to both the parents' houses to let them know. We won't know which of the boys it is until he is properly identified," he says, looking miserable.

I get off my knees and pull Dex away so we can talk in private.

"Doesn't it seem strange to you that he's in the same condition Aiden and the other boys were found in?" I remark, as I watch a member of the maritime crew cover the body with a blue tarpaulin sheet.

The boys I'm referring to are from previous missing cases I've investigated over the past two decades. Dex rolls his eyes; he's heard it all before. Every time they find a body in the harbour it brings me back to the mystery surrounding the murder of Aiden.

I know Dex and some of the other cops think I'm still bat shit crazy with anger over the death of my twin brother, and Dex also believes I have revenge on my mind. He is partly right. I still haven't gotten over my brother's death, and yes I seek revenge, but I also know the price I'd pay if I ever harmed the man who took Aiden and destroyed him. Over the years the thought has crossed my mind, what I would do to the monster that took my brother's life in such a heinous way. Sometimes I daydream about catching him, putting a gun in his mouth and pulling the trigger.

HORRORific Tales   (Cryptids)

****

On the day my world was wrenched apart it was a warm Saturday afternoon in 1990. I remember the sun was high in the sky, birds chirping loudly in the trees, the scent of Autumn hung thick in the air. After locking our bikes up to the rack, we headed inside. The day turned chilly after a couple of hours. We'd seen the Wolves and the Lions being fed. Walked around a bit. After a while we decided to sit on a patch of soft grass to eat the packed lunch I had in my backpack.

"I'm going to grab a coke; do you want anything?" Aiden asked.

"A lemonade," I replied, as I munched on a peanut butter sandwich.

I waited, and waited, but I got impatient and went looking for him. It was starting to drizzle. When I went to the kiosk, it was closed. I looked around and that is when I found Aiden's jacket lying in the shrubs. I raced as fast as I could to the reception desk to ask if anyone had seen him, but no one had. When I looked outside I saw that his bike was still next to mine; he would never have just left it and gone home without telling me.

"I'll call over the intercom, love. It'll be okay, don't worry. He's probably in the loo," Mrs Carter the receptionist said, trying to calm my frantic nerves.

"WOULD AIDEN BRADY PLEASE COME TO RECEPTION. YOUR SISTER IS WAITING FOR YOU," she called over the loudspeaker.

HORRORific Tales   (Cryptids)

By now I was nearly hyperventilating with worry. I could feel that something was wrong; a sense of dread enveloped me. Mrs Carter called the police and our parents, who arrived as daylight turned into night, and an immense darkness devoured the zoo. They searched everywhere, but they didn't find him.

Over the next few days, the sight of Aiden's face all over the news, compounded my grief. There were no solid leads. However, one of the zoo staff spoke to the police saying that he'd arrived at work the day Aiden went missing and spotted a white van idling in the NO PARKING zone. The driver having been described as possibly Māori or a Pacific Islander. Although the staff member had thought it was strange, he didn't think to mention it to anyone until the following day.

Aiden's bloated body was found a week later in Wellington harbour by someone walking their dog along Petone beach. I vividly recall hearing a cop delivering the news to my parents as I sat on the top of the staircase eavesdropping. It was mum's screams and wailing that had drawn me out of my bedroom.

Several weeks later, the coroner report had determined that Aiden had sustained multiple stab wounds, and his throat was viciously slashed open. There were marks on his wrists and ankles indicating that he had been bound with duct tape and possibly handcuffs or straps. He'd been found naked and had probably been submerged in the water for at least two days.

HORRORific Tales   (Cryptids)

The bite marks were impossible to identify, though it was noted as being from some type of aquatic animal and that it happened post-mortem.

Nightmares plagued me. *We're walking along the sand at Petone beach, laughing along to one of Aiden's stupid jokes. Next thing we're running away from something. Aiden is trying to catch up with me, but he is slowing down and I don't know why. All of a sudden, I see he is missing chunks from his body and his limbs are gone, and blood is pouring from the stumps; gushing over the sand, and turning the water red. A huge creature gnashes its serpent tail as it comes racing towards us at an impossible speed. All I see are a maw of teeth dragging my brother away. I'm frozen to the spot, screaming for help – but nobody comes…*

I'm not the type of person to believe in dreams having meanings, but I assess the creature in my nightmares is representative of the person who murdered Aiden.

As the weeks passed by, I kept asking myself. Why was Aiden taken and not me? I had so many unresolved questions but there was no one to talk to. My parents were too lost in their own grief, their own devastation to comfort me.

In the first few years, little things would trigger me, sending me spiralling back into the depths of misery. Hearing the music from the Mr Whippy ice-cream truck would have me buckled over. A rugby game on the TV reminded me too much of Aiden, I'd have to switch channels because he loved rugby and wanted to be an All Black one day, like his idol

HORRORific Tales (Cryptids)

Sean Fitzpatrick.

I never went back to the zoo. I never will.

Mum and dad eventually divorced a year after Aiden was murdered. I read somewhere that when a child dies under such terrible circumstances the parents of that child either band together in solace, or they break apart in sorrow.

The first few weeks back at school without Aiden was absolute hell. When something like this happens, people don't know what to say, so they say nothing at all. The kids would turn the other way when I walked into the classroom, and I could hear them whispering behind my back – I guess they thought my bad luck would rub off on them.

Although I tried to ignore it, I couldn't. I was a twelve-year-old child learning to navigate the world without my twin brother, and with little to no support. Even my best friend Megan abandoned me. I spent a lot of those years slumped in a deep dark depression.

Then one day my attitude changed. I began to obsess over the fucker that murdered Aiden. There had to be a way to solve this. I didn't want to let it go. My obsession grew larger, too large for me to hold it in anymore. I had to do something, so I made a huge decision that would change the trajectory of my life. I had a purpose.

HORRORific Tales (Cryptids)

At the age of twenty-two, I joined the police. My parents were proud. They'd managed to put aside their differences to attend my graduation at the police college in Porirua. I'd graduated top of my unit. My life was set.

I was going to hunt down my brother's killer.

******

Twenty-five years later, and now I am a detective with the CIB, based out of Wellington police station. I keep a photograph of Aiden on my desk. He is the reason I didn't give up or give in.

Dex and I are working on a case that involves two missing boys, Damien Russell and Sam Harris, both twelve-year-olds. They'd gone into the city to watch a movie at the Embassy Theatre, but they never returned home. After perusing through CCTV footage, we spotted a suspicious looking rusted white van rushing away from the back of the cinema with no licence plates and its lights off; even though it was 10:30pm.

It's been a few days since the boy was found in the harbour. The investigation is at a standstill until we receive confirmation as to the identity of the body.

I'm making a salad for dinner at home when Dex calls.

"What's up? Your wife kicked you out, and let me guess, you need my couch to sleep on again?"

"Haha, very funny, you should have been a comedian not a cop. The coroner just called and confirmed the body is Damien Russell."

I stop slicing through a mango, and put the knife down.

"Shit. Do his parents know yet?"

"Yes, they do. But we have a problem, they found another body in the harbour. No doubt this time it's Sam Harris. The water police confirmed that he has a large raspberry birthmark on his face. I've sent Arnie and Kate over to break the news to Sam's parents."

The following morning Dex and I are going over the case and what we know thus far. The suspect's modus operandi is that he targets only boys, he likes to leave his victims naked, stabbed to death, slashed throats and bound by their wrists and ankles. We might be looking for a dark-skinned male, possibly in his late 60s, who drives a white van. It'll be like looking for the proverbial needle in the haystack.

"Let's think logically about this Dex, there has to be a connection, right?" I say.

"You mean a connection to Aiden and the other boys? You think the boys were taken by the same person in the white van, and it is the same man who also took the boy in 2002, what was his name again?"

"Justin Slater, a thirteen-year-old. His body washed up in Shelly Bay, when he didn't return home from a bike ride," I reply.

"Oh yeah. Then there was that other one in 2015, Jeremy something," Dex states.

"Jeremy Baker, an eleven-year-old who vanished on his way to intermediate school," I reply.

"Your memory is amazing you know? And the two Miller brothers," he says.

"Kane and Eric Miller. That was in 2018. Twelve-year-old twin brothers. They went for a trek in the Remutaka Forest park and were found in the harbour a week later."

"Do you know how many white vans there are in the whole of the Wellington region?" he asks.

"No, but I guess you are about to tell me," I say, my voice dripping with sarcasm.

"Tens of thousands," he replies.

"We could start there though right? But then what if it's unregistered, it would be impossible to find," I say. "Dex I've been thinking. Why does he stop and start again after years of no activity? Where does he disappear to? Is he in prison serving out a lag for some other crime and reconvenes when he gets back out? Does he go overseas?"

"Very good observation. We'll have to look into that."

We aren't getting anywhere in the investigation to tell the truth. We've spoken to hundreds of people, and interviewed known sex offenders in the area, but they all have tight alibis.

HORRORific Tales   (Cryptids)

Although CCTV and door ring cameras are useful for investigations, because many people have opted for this type of security, we still can't get a definitive description of the perp or the van. As we are going through case files a mile high, because we are overlooking the previous similar cases, we get a phone call from the Sergeant. Dex picks up the landline and is speaking in low tones.

When he gets off the phone, his face is grim, and he's shaking his head – *this isn't good.*

"What's up? Did you get fired for being a shit lazy cop?"

"Not funny Jules. There have been reports of body parts washed up along Petone beach. I don't know what's going on, but we've all been called in to assist. They'll brief us when we get out there."

"And where is there exactly?" I ask.

"Petone, down by the wharf," he states, looking like he's eaten something rotten.

We pull up to the scene and they have already setup a marquee. When we get inside the Sergeant pulls us aside. He shows us what they've found. There is a boot with a foot still inside it. A hand missing some of its digits. A few other unmentionables that shouldn't be outside a human body. They're lined up along a makeshift table, and the scene is so grotesque, I run out and vomit in the bush.

It takes me back to the day of Aiden's funeral, where we had to have a closed casket because they didn't find all of him, and the state of his body; my parents didn't want anyone to see him in that condition.

"Are you okay?" Dex asks.

"I'm fine." I spit, as I wave him away.

"Give yourself a few minutes and join us when you can," he says patting my back.

He walks away, and I pace up to the water's edge. It's the same body of water where they found my brother, all those years ago. I can't escape it. We are all connected to this harbour, one way or another.

As minutes turn into hours and the sun drifts slowly across the sky, we wait but we aren't of any real use here. There've been no further reports of body parts washed upon the shore, but it doesn't mean there won't be any more.

The case has turned into a monumental nightmare, where we are chasing our tails, around and around in circles, where absolutely nothing makes sense, and I can't see an end in sight.

"Let's get over to the morgue. There's no use us sitting here twiddling our thumbs," I suggest.

"Yes, let's go there and see what they have come up with," Dex agrees.

Silence fills the car as we drive to Wellington hospital where the morgue is located. The sun feels warm on my face as I watch the world pass by outside the car window. I'm consumed with memories of Aiden, until I'm snapped from my reverie when the Sergeant calls, diverting us in the opposite direction, back out to a suburb in the Hutt Valley.

HORRORific Tales (Cryptids)

"Officer Stevens is out on a job and needs back up, said he can smell decomposition. Can you head out there? Neighbours in the area called it in."

We speed along the motorway, lights flashing, sirens blaring.

In my mind the thoughts of Aiden intensify. Images of his face flash before me, along with a montage of childhood memories. A deep sorrow digs its way inside my head, and unrelenting feelings of despair shoot through my core, but I don't know why – it feels like I'm being pulled towards Aiden, like some invisible thread is connecting us. I'm snapped back to the present moment when we finally arrive at the location.

"Hey, what's up?" I ask Stevens. "Sergeant said you smelt decomposition? It sure as hell stinks like an abattoir out here, though it's probably a hunter," I say sniffing the air, and wishing that I hadn't.

"Yes it's putrid," Stevens replies.

There are houses everywhere, with huge backyards, sheds, other makeshift out buildings; the stench could be coming from anywhere.

"Look, how about we split up and try and see where it's coming from? Knock on some doors, and if we have no luck, we can call one of the K9 units in," I suggest.

Officer Stevens goes to the house we pulled up in front of, Dex walks over to the house on the right, and I meander over to the house on the left. The gate is hanging on one hinge; it scrapes the concrete, making a hideous noise. The garden is a tangled mess, and the house is rundown. Plywood cover the windows, and the stench of decay is getting stronger.

I bang on the door, announcing, "Police, can you come to the door please?"

I knock several times until finally the door opens a crack. A Māori man with grey hair peeks through the gap.

"Good afternoon. I'm Detective Julia Brady. Is there a chance we can have a chat?"

"What do you want?" the man asks abruptly.

His old diluted brown eyes keep looking over my

head and out towards Stevens squad car.

"What's your name please?" I ask.

"Walter. What's this about?"

"We're looking around the area as there's been a report of an offensive stench. Are you a hunter by any chance?"

"Yes, I have a shed out back, you can probably smell the buck my buddies and I killed in the weekend," he says.

"Can I take a look in your shed please?"

He hesitates and glances back over his shoulder.

"Of course, come in while I grab the keys."

I follow him inside. He closes the front door. In the hallway he tells me to wait, but I get impatient and drift into the living room. I am stopped dead in my tracks when I see pinned to one entire wall are photographs of children. Upon closer inspection, I see Damien Russell, Sam Harris, and numerous other boys I also recognise. It's when I see the picture of Aiden that I swiftly take my 9mm Glock out of my holster belt.

I feel sick in my gut, and I want to throw up.

Looking around I notice an altar on the other side of the room. I sneak over to investigate. Red and white candles spread a sickly scent that swirls around me like a serpent. Shivers lace my back when I see who the tribute is to. There are sketches of a taniwha, a mythical creature from Māori folklore. There is something about the taniwha that has my skin crawling, like millions of fire ants are biting me from the inside out. It's a massive black reptilian creature that looks like a dragon without wings.

My head feels foggy as I try to remember where I have seen these before. The more I think, the faster the thought dissipates. Then it hits me. I know about this taniwha. I learnt about it in the Māori legends course I did at college. It is said that Hine-kōrako was a beautiful Māori princess, but she fell in love with a warrior from a warring tribe. Her father, the chief of the village was not happy about their courting. So, in his fury, he turned her into a sea creature, so that she could never be with her true love. It is believed that her love wanders the beach in search of her every night.

I am so lost in thought, that I don't hear the noise behind me until it is too late. Something smashes hard into the back of my skull.

I wake on the floor and Walter is standing above me pointing a gun in my face. I reach for my gun, but it's gone.

"You shouldn't be here!" he yells, kicking me hard in the side of my body. I curl into a ball to protect myself.

When I see the spectral apparition of Aiden standing in the corner of the room, dressed in the clothes he went missing in, that's when I realise I'm about to die. Now I'm never going to get justice for my brother after all. It's all been for nothing!

"Walter, stop! Let me go, please," I beg, as hot tears slide down the side of my face.

"No! You don't understand!" Walter yells, as the gun trembles in his hand.

"I understand enough to know you murdered innocent boys for your sick and demented pleasure. You took my brother away from me!" I scream, spittle flying from my mouth.

"You don't get it. Let me explain," he demands.

"What the hell are you talking about?" I ask, my voice shivering.

"I am appeasing the creature in the harbour. Her name is Hine-kōrako. One day, my wife Kiri and our son Tama. We were swimming at Days Bay beach. That is when I first saw Hine the taniwha. She was trying to take my son, so I ran in after him. As I tried to pull him free, Hine spoke to me, but I don't know how, perhaps telepathically. I swore to her that day, if she let my Tama go unharmed, I would bring her more victims.

She let him go, and ever since I have been feeding her. She'd said if I keep her well fed, she would continue to let my son live. I had to, I just had to do it!"

I watch him closely to gage the situation. Either this man is bonkers, or it could explain the mysterious bite marks found on each of the victims' bodies.

"You don't believe me," he says, kicking me in the gut. "We can't stop her, if I don't feed her, she might come out of the water and ravage the city, like she said she would. We can't let that happen. It's been getting worse, she wants more. So, sometimes I have to give her two!"

"That's bullshit and you know it!" I say, as he picks me up by the hair, with the gun pointed at my head. "You're delusional! You need help. Tell me, why do you stop and start again, I need to know," I cry out.

"Oh, you want to know that? Well, I haven't stopped, I have been doing this every week for the past twenty-five years. Some of the boys you will never find, because I saw Hine gobble them up whole."

I think I must be dreaming when I see Dex standing in the doorway with his gun aimed at Walter.

"Back away now, before I blow your fucking head off," Dex screams at Walter.

Aiden glides closer. Walter puts his pistol on the floor.

"Kick it towards the detective," Dex directs the monster from my nightmares.

As soon as the gun is in my reach, I grab it and stand lightning quick, too fast for Dex to stop me. I put the barrel of the gun inside the mouth of the man who murdered my brother. I flick the safety switch and I'm about to pull the trigger, when Aiden approaches me. Inside my mind I hear him telling me not to do it.

"Jules, put the gun down. This isn't justice. You'll end up in jail, and you'll lose your job. We can take him in alive and make him pay that way," Dex tries to convince me.

"No, I want to do it! I have to do it! I don't care about jail, fuck that, I have to end his life, it's all I have. It's what I have been waiting for my entire life."

Aiden is standing beside me now, shaking his head.

"Trust me, if Aiden were here, he wouldn't want you to do this!"

The gun is shaking in my hands. I hear steel crunching against teeth. Aiden approaches me and touches my hand…though I can't feel him. Only for Aiden, I take the gun out of Walter's mouth. He crumples to the floor, and Dex snaps handcuffs on the man who ruined my life. I watch on slightly detached from the situation, as Aiden waves me goodbye.

HORRORific Tales   (Cryptids)

A bright light breaches the ceiling and I watch, with swollen eyes, as he travels up through the light and disappears.

The crime scene unit arrive and Walter is put into Stevens police car. When they look inside the shed, they find chains attached to the walls, boxes of duct tape, a variety of knives, and other tools. A huge buck is hanging from the ceiling, rotting; if it wasn't for that animal, I don't think we would have found Walter.

On the day Walter Logan is convicted for the murder of twelve boys; even though we know there are more victims, I visit Aiden's grave, say goodbye, and leave behind one of his teddy bears I've been holding onto all of these years. Dex is patting my back.

"Come on, let's go before it pisses down. What's next for you?" Dex asks.

"I've already handed in my resignation, and I think I might treat myself to a vacation, somewhere warm," I say as we walk away from the cemetery, away from Aiden.

The sun comes out and lightens the way to my future. My goal is complete, I found the man who murdered Aiden. I smile, life is great. I feel lighter now I know my brother is finally at peace.

But I have another mission to do, by myself. I need to track down the taniwha, to see if what Walter says is true, that a taniwha lives in Wellington harbour, and if we don't stop it, it could come for us all.

HORRORific Tales   (Cryptids)

Follow Del's work here:

A (Jersey) Devil of a Time Back in November '77

by
Anthony M Caro

HORRORific Tales   (Cryptids)

Here we are, me and three of my friends, Chris, who you know. Eye-twitching Paul. And hefty Georgie.

Okay. You might not know Chris personally, but you knew kids like him in high school.

That was quite a 1977 November night for me, the boys, Chris, and the Jersey Devil.

Chris. He's the star. Not me. Not Paul. Not Georgie. Not the folks who spray-painted pentagrams on the unoccupied looney bin's walls. Not the Jersey Devil.

I like Chris. Chris is a goof. God bless him. He's goofy in a lot of ways. One of the ways he's goofy is he takes those stupid books we read in grade school seriously. No, I don't mean the First Feathers "learn to read" tome. I mean those crackpot Bigfoot and Abominable Snowman books.

Chris read all of them.

For a New Jersey boy, Chris had a love for Bigfoot. You'd think you'd have to be from California to love some Bigfoot. In 1967, you had to travel far to see a hairy beastie, if you could see a hairy beastie. By 1977, Bigfoot was everywhere.

That made Bigfoot boring.

New Jersey called its resident hairy creature Big Red Eye to deflect away from the absurd notion America's Abominable Snowman was hanging out slightly south of Newark. Big Red Eye's sightings played the B-side. New Jersey had its headlining mysterious monster.

Head like a horse. Hooves like a goat. Body like a kangaroo. Wings like everything else with wings. Fans, the glorious state of New Jersey brings you…THE Jersey Devil.

Bringing it to ya' via bar room banter.

Once Chris found out New Jersey had experienced a series of horrifying sightings back in 1909, not too different from all the Bigfoot mayhem of the 1970s, he had to search for as much information as he could about the Jersey Devil, a long-time resident cryptid of the Garden State. Popular here. Middling everywhere else.

Bigfoot = The Beatles.

Loch Ness Monster = The Rolling Stones.

The Jersey Devil = Herman's Hermits.

HORRORific Tales (Cryptids)

The Jersey Devil had his time in the sun, and it passed. (The dubious 1955 comeback excluded.)

Chris believed in the Jersey Devil. Like others, he started obsessing when he read about it in a book chronicling friends of a friend's tales supporting the first-person friend of a friend's tales he heard in person about the weird beast.

How many people believed in the local monster? More than you think, although more people believed Satanists perform evil rituals in old, abandoned asylums. But what are the odds you'll run into Satanists when trespassing in one?

While not many high school kids thought it was real, a group of high school kids with one friend left of center (mentally, not politically) knew the Jersey Devil was resting, awaiting his next reign of mayhem, and rousing him wouldn't be too hard. We sold trespassing into a decrepit former hotel for the clinically insane at 3 AM to Chris this way.

If you pull aside and speak to him in person as a friend, he tells you the odds of finding a Bigfoot were much better than seeing a Jersey Devil. One thing works in favor of proving humanoid apes on two legs exist - their purported population. The Jersey Devil? There's only one. Singularity makes him much more challenging to find.

Plus, he's exclusive to New Jersey. Bigfoot branched out nationally a long time ago.

Locally, you'd find me and the boys ready to play a high school prank on Chris. What you wouldn't see was the Jersey Devil. You wouldn't find a Big Red Eye, meaning you wouldn't find a Bigfoot. Not an official one. You'd find the Big Red Eye, as in the one Georgie made of himself. Husky Georgie squeezed himself into the $14.99 gorilla costume we ordered from a magazine mercifully delivered on time.

An uninhabited mental facility four hundred yards from the highway is something you'd find. We found it. If you stuck your head inside that joint in November '77, you'd find us.

If you stood where I stood, you'd find me, Paul, and Georgie, although you might not recognize Georgie easily since he's wearing the gorilla suit.

Chris? You would find him easily. If you went down the stairs, turned right, headed down the hallway, turned left, waltzed down the second hallway, and went down more stairs. You would see a goofy-looking kid holding a somewhat functional 16 mm camera there—no Super 8 stuff. No, Chris wanted a

HORRORific Tales (Cryptids)

16mm deal. He wanted it so bad he broke into the school after dark to steal one from the AV club. (They never locked the windows at the school.)

Can you blame him for taking a risk? Suppose you're going through the trouble of raising the Jersey Devil from his (presumed) resting place in a ditched mental shack and want to get it on film. A semi-professional 16mm camera is a better choice than a home movie job.

Yeah, once we wake up the winged menace from where he's been resting since 1909 (or 1955), we'll run him past Chris, who will catch the whole thing on film.

We should've stolen our own cameras. A 35mm one. No. 70mm. Cinemascope. In SUPER 3-D.

I kid. We never intended to film a Jersey Devil; we wanted to film the look on Chris' face when Big Red Eye ran past him.

A little background - Chris does okay in high school. I'm failing. Paul's hanging on. George is ready to be held back again. The three of us collectively used our marginal high school education to come up with this ridiculous prank.

Unfortunately, we ignored those friend-of-a-friend Satanic ritual tales. New Jersey myths don't mention Satanists performing rituals in the abandoned mental asylums for nothing.

Not that they show up in asylums every night, and what would be the odds they would show up in the mental asylum the same night we show up?

Turns out pretty darn good.

I must tell you things didn't go as we thought they would. I should've been smarter back in 1977.

The damn Jersey Devil was locked up for 68 years. That's why so few people saw him. During a rash of alleged sightings in 1955, the state police posted signs suggesting the "Jersey Devil is a hoax," so we won't count '55. 1909 was the first and last stellar year of the Jersey Devil. I guess.

Not really. Sightings happen all the time.

"Hmghmmmhgh," Georgie retorted. It wasn't easy to understand him because of the distance and chosen attire of a gorilla suit. The mask was oversized, so we wrapped some duct tape to keep it tighter, making it hard to hear Georgie.

Georgie. He was a big guy. Oh, he was still a dork. When you're a dork over six feet and 250 lbs. People who pick on you get slapped around. Not tonight. Poor Georgie.

HORRORific Tales (Cryptids)

"Hmghmmmhgh," Georgie reiterated. At least, that's what it sounded like from 20 feet away. Or should I say from 20 feet above? He might not be hanging from those ropes from a full 20 feet, but it's high enough.

Did I mention he's hanging upside down, and the Satanists wrapped the rope around his feet? I should point out he's hanging over a pentagram drawn on the concrete floor.

"Hmghmmmhgh," he cried.

Tragic Paul. I almost forgot about him. He's cowering in the corner. I can't blame him for cowering. He's been hog-tied by the half dozen Satanists crashing our little prank. They gagged him, not realizing he doesn't talk much. He moves his eyes a lot when he isn't sure whether to go along with one of our schemes. Call it a nervous tick. Those eyes are moving back and forth rapidly now.

Paul lived on the edge of being an outcast or working his way up to the High School B crowd. He had more fun being an outcast with us. Poor Paul.

We need to make a checklist of all the urban legends and myths.

Satanists.

Big Red Eye (aka Bigfoot in all but name)

Abandoned mental asylum.

Jersey Devil. (Unconfirmed.)

That's a lot going on for a little state like New Jersey. Bigger states don't even remotely have as many myths. The Pacific Northwest of Northern California, all of Oregon, all of Washington, and an undetermined amount of British Columbia have their Sasquatches but little else. I'm not going to count ghosts or UFOs. They belong in a different book.

New Jersey has everything the 48, Hawaii, and Alaska have, and more.

"More" being the Jersey Devil, who gets a little attention outside the southern part of the state.

I'm sure California has abandoned mental asylums somewhere. It's a hell of a big state. I doubt it has as many as the state of New Jersey. California likely had more but demolished them. NJ has little interest in doing anything with them. So, they remain standing for time eternity like fifth-rate pyramids.

HORRORific Tales (Cryptids)

What can you do in a deserted sanitarium? If you're not a high schooler looking to pull a prank, you could try to raise the Jersey Devil from the grave. But only if you're a Satanist.

Paul, all hog-tied, sat next to a bloated weekend warrior Satanist with a big belly and an even bigger axe.

They gag him, so all he can say is, "Mmmmmmph," a variant of the dialect of "Hmghmmmhgh," upside-down Georgie mutters.

At least they make more sense than the Top-Dog Satanist. He's prone to say, "Elllere mazaas ong kom go hou!" That's what it sounds like to me. Doesn't make much sense until he pulls out the big knife from under his robe. The other Satanists start to chant something equally incoherent, but the knife adds coherency to the point of their commentary.

Chris, buddy, please don't walk up the flight of stairs either by yourself or with the camera.

I didn't buy the rumors of Satanists using cast-aside mental asylums for their nefarious deeds. I paid no attention to Big Red Eye sightings. I didn't care how often some news magazine reported on Bigfoot or an old Bigfoot movie, which shows up on television at 1 AM. I definitely paid no attention to the Jersey Devil sightings rumors. Too local. Bigfoot/Bigfeet was/were (a) national star(s).

The Satanist stuff I did vaguely care about. Becoming a Satanist involves nothing more than declaring oneself a Satanist. The whole performing rituals in a long-forsaken sanitarium. This was something I thought never happened.

Who has that kind of time on their hands? Turns out - five. One has an axe.

The best-robed of the five sports a nasty dagger - a dagger placed on Georgie's throat.

"Hmghmmmhgh," went Georgie.

Such hoopla for a C-level monster. Where'd he come from?

HORRORific Tales   (Cryptids)

Old Mother Leeds. Poor woman. She had so many children she didn't know what to do. "Let it be a devil!" she cried. Cry some more, she did, when the deformed Leeds devil crawled out of the womb and flew out up the chimney and out into the world back in 1735.

People have been seeing the Jersey Devil ever since. Some even sober. Others claim the devil died a long time ago and has been resting in a secret burial place awaiting resurrection by devil fans.

Who believes that shit?

At a minimum, five Satanists.

No more "Hmghmmmhgh-ing" from Georgie. He replaced it with "Gaaaagack!" when the Top-Dog Satanist Priest dragged the dagger across his throat.

Damn sharp dagger. It cut through the thick fake gorilla fur and did a number on Georgie's throat. Fake gorilla fur is apparently not absorbent. Blood flowed from his costume to the pentagram on the concrete floor below him.

"Malagenio. Conzakk. Eperno del' lioffo," uttered the Top-Dog Satanist as he slowly pulled the knife across Georgie's throat. You could hear fabric and fake fur ripping when the dagger cut across the gorilla costume's neckline. It sounded like someone cutting a carpet - if a carpet also let out gurgling sounds.

"Ziozo, montaka, rah," continued the Top-Dog Satanist. He spoke the incantation intended to bring the Jersey Devil from his resting place.

This raises a question: how does the Jersey Devil understand what the Top-Dog is saying?

The Jersey Devil is from New Jersey. We don't speak that bullshit here.

Blood swirled in puddles over the pentagram. We all waited. I wondered how long they'd wait until the Jersey Devil pulled a predictable no-show. Devils and demons never show up for the weekend warriors.

Do I smell sulfur and brimstone? Do I see smoke coming from the puddles of blood on the ground? Those cracks in the floor mean this place either has a bad foundation….

HORRORific Tales   (Cryptids)

A deformed goat's hoof breaks through a piece of cement.

….or the Jersey Devil's reliable.

Time stops for a second before large chunks of a concrete floor start breaking apart. A hoof burst through the concrete and it's hard to tell what kind of creature the hoof belonged to. Is it a horse? Is it a goat? Once the bizarre creature pulled itself out of the hole, I stopped debating where the head came from and realized everyone was right about the torso. The dress size absolutely fits a kangaroo.

I freeze in shock, but not enough that my senses can't tell what the smoke coming from the Jersey Devil's nostrils is by the smell of pure sulfur. Looks like some of those reports from the sightings were spot-on.

You'd think he'd be happy to rise from his tomb. When are creatures unhappy about rising from their tomb? The look on his horsehead face displays pure rage. Time stalls as the Jersey Devil sizes up the messy scenario.

He looks at cowering Paul, throat-slit Georgie, and a long stare at frozen me. The slapdash creature's eyes squint, and it turns to look at the Satanists.

Mother Leed's devilish offspring didn't move except for mild wing flapping. The wings moved slightly while faint sulfur smoke drifted from his nostrils. Then, he made a decision and his move.

The wings flapped hummingbird-fast, and the weird Garden State *l'enfant terrible* darted in the Satanists' direction,

He's one of the good guys.

The Top-Dog Satanist could barely raise his dagger before he had blood pouring out of his throat. Those wings are sharp, and the Jersey Devil knows how to use them. The creature beelines toward the guy with the axe. Fear messed up his aim because he swung the ax and ended up lopping off Paul's head - right before the obese Satanist lost his own.

Three Satanists left. Then two. I had to turn my head away from the slaughter. Admittedly, the sounds of footsteps also drew my attention. Those footsteps were coming up from the stairs.

Chris.

With a 16mm camera in tow.

HORRORific Tales   (Cryptids)

I turned back to look at the scene, and it was like when someone tugged at your shirt, and you turned to see who did it, but nobody was there. Then, you look down and see a small child. If you look further down to the floor, you'll see five bloody Satanist corpses. Looking up toward the ceiling, you'd see the Jersey Devil flapping its wings.

The Jersey Devil stared at a dumbfounded, frozen Chris for barely two seconds before beelining its path toward the now-open stairwell door.

Chris displayed the necessary grit to be a monster hunter in the 1970s. He overcame his shock quickly to pull the trigger on the 16mm camera's shutter. The camera's mechanical chatter sound filled the mostly silent room. The only other thing breaking the silence was the sound of blood dripping on the floor.

The camera filmed about three to five seconds of the open doorway as Chris snapped back to attention, then panned left to capture the scene from eye level. Chris slowly tilted the camera down to the bloody floor, panning to capture the dismembered body parts.

Clack.

The camera made such a sound when Chris took his finger off the trigger. The whirring stopped.

Chris remained silent and expressionless, saying nothing until he suggested, "We should take a walk to the payphone we passed on the highway."

Back then, you had to walk to a payphone to call someone, but only if you had a dime, the receiver would accept a collect call, or the call was free. Calling the cops was free. Calling them served as the perfect excuse to get out of the damned place.

I couldn't tell you how many abandoned mental asylums there are in New Jersey today. Technically, there are no occupied mental asylums in New Jersey today. They call them psychiatric hospitals. I have no idea how many psychiatric hospitals there are in New Jersey today, but I can confirm one has a comfortable bed and relatively decent food. The comforts and cuisine improved slowly but surely over the decades.

Chris sleeps in a more comfortable bed and eats finer cuisine in a place far away from New Jersey. He did well with the books, speaking fees, and movie rights. He made good money lying about the Jersey Devil.

HORRORific Tales   (Cryptids)

When the cops, media, and everyone else reviewed the blurry, out-of-focus 16mm film of a "winged creature" flying in and out of frame, they asked Chris what it was. He glanced at the state police officer's holstered revolvers and, following the advice in those old monster books about protecting these rare creatures, he lied with a straight face. "It's a trick of shadows, light, and an angry goose." New Jersey has plenty of geese, angry, content, and indifferent.

They asked me, and I told them the truth. I've been telling the truth about all those bodies and the Jersey Devil for years. Chris knows it's true. He's lying.

Or is he playing a prank on me?

Follow Anthony and his work here:

Elijah's Shadow

by
Justine Johnston Hemmestad

HORRORific Tales   (Cryptids)

What has been lurking in the shadows, beneath giant cliffs and between trees taller and older than he, since before the existence of humanity? *He* has, his giant feet firmly etched from the earth, his broad body evasive to the will of evolution. He is unmistakable but deceptive at the same time. No one can deny his existence, yet he would never let them find proof that he still lives, or they would surely kill him.

He scratches his head, his fingers enveloped by the expanse of his own hair, and he wonders how to stay unseen in the shadows of the forest. He's determined to stay as he is, even as the world changes around him. He knows his brothers have built civilizations in the years they've been in this land, just as they did in their birth land. He also knows they've forgotten their feats at home. They've forgotten home all together. They are a people of unknown origin.

If they had remembered, they wouldn't hide who they really are by hating who he is. Truly, they would embrace who they are – they would allow their innate light shine from their eyes. But he, Elijah, has the will and the power to ward off the single-mindedness of change. While his brothers run from who they are by building monument after monument and road after road, he has faced who he is. He has held onto his history, a time greater than any time that had come since. But his brethren wouldn't know it – they were deceived by their fear of themselves.

He could only love his brethren from afar. They did not accept who they had once been, and they would never accept him as he is. So, he would forever roam the earth for he is dominant over the earth. Those who stalk him in their fear of him will never know that he has the power to change their paths. There is nothing he does not have dominion over. He's bigger and faster than any other creature like him – for he is the physical outer fringes of the Creator Himself. Yet, only one thing has ever threatened his existence.

With nowhere else to go but where he is, he does not know any other way of life. His brethren roam the forest in search of him to kill him because he refuses to give in to the change, and there's nothing he can do to thwart his brethren. He has no one to reason with, no one to remember him. He raises his right hand, covered in hair, and extends his finger to the mountains in front of him, mesmerized by the bolt of electricity that shot out through his fingertips. Why would he want to change when he has power such as this at his fingertips? He couldn't understand why his brothers changed without regret.

HORRORific Tales   (Cryptids)

But if his brethren saw, as they cut down the trees with their saws, they would kill Elijah out of fear. There would be no words exchanged, for his brethren are too afraid of him. If his brethren had courage, Elijah of course would not be alone. If his brethren had strength, they would put down their saws and let the trees live, for out of the trees comes the breath of life. Even his brethren's daughters would not fear him, if his brethren had courage

But they hide in their inventions and their falsities. Not him. He remembered seeing the great lighthouse in Alexandria, the sacrifices at the temple in Jerusalem, and even the flood that had once engulfed the world. He hadn't forgotten those things, nor had he forgotten who he was and what he had the power to do.

He raised his leathery face toward the sun and inhaled deeply, his lungs withstanding the pollen that rode in with the air. A flock of birds flew out of the trees – and away from *him*. He had to keep moving, that he knew. He remembered streets made of stone, the fires blazing on their edges, the horse hooves clomping. He remembered the statues of false gods, the flowers spread out before them, and he knew he had to keep moving. He would never allow his mind to become so complacent as it had been in the land of his birth.

Barreling through the crowded trees, Elijah remembers his own name - but he doesn't use it. There's no one to use it with. The biggest hindrance to remaining the same is watching the distance grow between his brethren and himself. As they searched the woods for him, they did not remember his name. This terrifies him. No one else that he catches a glimpse of has ever used his name; instead, his brothers use made-up names to refer to him. He knows he's alone.

But Elijah has not forgotten his brothers. He knows they are only afraid of him because they do not recognize him. And they are afraid of themselves because they were once like him. They could not stomach the light that emulated from their fingertips. They had diminished themselves, and now they wanted to diminish *him*.

So the mountains are his home, the trees his sanctuary – even when they hunt him. Even when they think they catch him on their memory recorders, he evades them and he always will.

HORRORific Tales   (Cryptids)

He remembers when they were like him – everyone in the land of his birth blanketed with hair over their bodies as though covered in the embrace of the Creator, everyone twice the height of what his brothers had lessened themselves to be now; everyone with long arms to reach to higher lengths. Now, his brothers did not need longer-reaching arms to be like every other being who had diminished themselves. He wondered why they would ever diminish themselves.

Elijah came with his brothers when they travelled over the vast, seemingly endless waters to this new land - but he was the only one among them who could not see the good in the change they sought. As soon as they landed upon the shores of this land, they began digging for something they didn't have – as though they were determined to have an Egypt with them everywhere they went. This was their limitation.

Instead of appreciating themselves, retaining what they knew to be perfect about themselves, they gave into the change around them. That change smoothed their faces and their skin, straightened their backs, shortened their arms, and drew them out of the forests. They began to populate the land and build civilizations. And they remained in such inner darkness that they wanted to change everyone they stumbled upon in their own image. Even Elijah.

But he found that if he stayed in the forests, they would forget him. Their intuitive eyes were closed, their instinct was lost to convention. He could live freely as he was, as he was created to be, and resist the change of his brothers. They searched for what they once had and they did not know it. If only they could remember that they were once as rich in life as he is.

He has stomped far enough down the mountainside to watch them in their limited humanity. He witnessed their attempt at organized language – they had to voice their words, when before their change there was only thought and instinct. They knew one another deeply. Words distanced them from each other and completely tore them away from *him*. They had not stayed in the brilliant light that was naturally within them, the light that Elijah emulated at will.

In their fear of the light, Elijah's brethren slowly morphed into something less holy. What they feared, they killed. He knows that; he sees it happen. That is why he knows he has to remain hidden from them. They brought their own plague of depression and darkness with them out of Egypt. Indeed, he had never been so alone since they had arrived in this land.

HORRORific Tales   (Cryptids)

He roamed the mountainsides – *alone*. No one else had chosen not to change. No one else appreciated their original selves. He breathes deeply, as he takes long strides from tree to tree in isolation, feeling the ground sink with each step. He knows they'll kill him if they see him, and he lives with that. The only protection he has is to stay in the mountains.

Sometimes he sings to honor the Creator…the One he loves so much, the One he traveled over the waters to be near…the One he knows loves him. There is no need to change when the goal of his life is to be loved by his Creator. He lives in caves and secret dwellings and sings to the Creator at night when no one hears him. The Creator's lights shine through the sky and embrace him – and he knows he's right not to change.

There has to be others in the world who have not changed like him, but he does not know where to find them. Surely, some of those who stayed behind in the homeland have not changed. Even with the threat of the enormous creatures that sent them searching for a new land to begin with.

Elijah shakes his head free of the memories, rattling the land upon which he stands. Every time he moves the trees are shaken; every time he takes a step the world feels it. He deeply affects his surroundings, from each tiny, winged insect, to the frequent deer that dash past him. How could his brothers have given up that power to move the world with a single step? How could they think it was normal to diminish the light within them? Elijah would never understand. So, loneliness was a price he was willing to pay if it meant he would remain how the Creator made him. Hand-sculpted, was how he longed to remain.

He stands behind a tree trunk as wide as his shoulders in order to stay hidden from the sight of his brethren. They seem to be determined to get closer to him, to reach him, when he knows they would only torment him. It is not Elijah who threatens them – but they who threaten Elijah.

His brethren bring guns and bright lights, lights that do not shine from within, but lights that are artificially made from what they perceive to be their own genius. They rely on themselves and everything they can make to live and to force their beliefs onto him. Even now, millennia later.

HORRORific Tales   (Cryptids)

He was silent behind the tree – if there was one thing he knew how to do in the present times, it was to remain hidden from his brethren. But he couldn't stay here forever, he needed to move on. He needed to keep moving, always. Though he did not accept their change, he hadn't stopped moving forward.

The stone steps of their homeland are mountains in this distant land. His brethren had worn armor in his homeland, though here they had worn leather and feathers in their hair through the years. The strong scent of myrrh was replaced by the scent of sage in this land, though the smoke still streamed into the nostrils of his brethren no matter which land they were in.

Sometimes the peace induced by the scent makes him long to reach out from his hiding places and touch those who burned incense. Thoughts dash through his mind that one day he might not be alone. Then he remembers that his brethren wants to kill him, and he also remembers that he's not alone, for the Creator is with him.

Then it happens - his hiding place is discovered. Elijah hears the shrill scream of one of his brethren, and he knows he has been seen. They fear who they really are.

"Stay away from me!" she screams.

Elijah tells her not to fear him, though his plea surely sounds like a grunt to his brethren. How could languages be heard when ideologies were so feared?

He remembers the arrows of his homeland, much like the arrows used in recent times in this land, and he wonders if her scream is equipped with such lethalness. Her voice has already shattered his soul. He could continue to roam the woods, even sail the world again, and still the pain of her voice will forever be an injury to his soul. He wishes he could tell her to stop screaming in a language she understands. But her eyes, purple and devastating, pierce him almost deeper than her voice.

She is one of his brethren. She had changed like the rest of them who feared who they were. Judging by her fear, she is without the memory of the fall of Babel. But Elijah remembers how deeply each of his brethren who died building the tower had stricken him. Like her scream. He remembers the deadening thuds of their bodies as they hit the ground in plums of dust, much like his heart with her scream.

HORRORific Tales   (Cryptids)

He shakes his head, but he's sure his gesture isn't as clear to her as it feels to himself. He holds his palms out toward her in a motion to quiet her screams. He lived without words in his homeland, though his brethren lived *with* words in this land. Since she lives with them, he wonders if she'll ever understand him. Surprising him though, she suddenly stops screaming.

Her lips quiver; her hands rose and press against the sides of her head. Her long black hair glistens in the single stream of moonlight that pierces through the canopy of treetops. Her hair looks so soft to him, like the beds of silk that the Creator had first lain out for him and his brethren. But as he remembers, he soon recognizes the fear that creeps into her eyes again. He knows he has to do something to help her remember too. He has to jolt her out of her ignorance.

He gently tells her the story of his birth in a distant land beyond the sea, but she takes a sharp breath and very slowly and deliberately tries to inch away from him, beyond the trees. She must think that if she moves slowly enough, he won't notice until she is free. He can't allow her to leave without enlightening her to the truth of who she is though.

Elijah picks up a fallen branch and cuts the ground with it, much like he once etched lines into stone to tell a story in his homeland. Can he tell the story well enough now to help her remember? He isn't sure. He tries to draw lines like he once had drawn them on stone, but he knows that language is lost. So, he draws a bird, and he draws waves, and he draws the sun. Will it be enough to make her understand he's come from a distant land…just like her, before she changed to conform with the world in all its complacency?

He tries to sing the songs of his birth land to her. She can't hear them. He knows she can't hear their depth and their romance because she turns partially, as though she may attempt to flee. Yet, he stops her with his silence, and by meeting her gaze. He would communicate with her through his own language, if he could not communicate with her through hers. He could feel his heart melting in his longing to make her understand him. He knows she has to feel it because she winces, and even takes a bold step toward him, the small rocks shifting loudly beneath her shoe.

The wind picks up through the trees, shifting the fur on his body in an eerie way – but he pushes that thought from his mind; he wants her to remember with him.

HORRORific Tales (Cryptids)

He thought of the Creator's intent as he formed him – as though the Creator's intent and his intent were the same. Nothing pleases Elijah more than to be in unison with his Creator and he wants her to feel that.

She takes a quiet, soft step toward him, her long hair shifting over her shoulders, her clothes tightening at the bends of her limbs. She breathes steadily now, along with his thoughts. He can feel her lungs fill with air, then release her fear. He's mindful of time and decides it's too soon to reach out to her or to make the land upon which she stands glow with the light that could emulate from his fingertips.

Instead, she reaches her small hand toward him and lightly touches his arm. She doesn't seem to be afraid any longer and he treasures her courage. Her screams are stifled by understanding. He knows she's remembering him, and that she realizes she's like him even though she can not see it as clearly yet as he did. He knows she speaks with a voice like his brethren, though he hears her compassion in his heart in the same language he speaks to her with.

"I'm not afraid of you," she whispers into his heart. He feels the warmth of tears well up in his eyes. No one has opened up to him like that since the land of his birth. She is receptive to his voice; she listens to him and hears him.

"I am glad," Elijah's heart whispers back. He knows he's broken through the greatest barrier of his life.

Then a deafening gunshot crackles through the woods. She jumps back and screams, though not at the sight of him this time but with fear of the shooter, whom she cannot yet see.

Her gaze darts back to Elijah, and she screams again – this time louder than any scream that has met his ears before. And she's not looking into his eyes, but at his stomach.

He looks down and sees the blood seeping out of his flesh and dripping from the ends of his hair. And a thin stream of white smoke arose from the piercing. He doesn't feel the pain at first – then when he does, he knows there is nothing he can do but run away. There's no more time. The piercing of his heart, when he knows he'll never see her again is worse than any death could be. Yet, he promised the Creator life, so he knows he must live. He would not live if he stayed with her.

HORRORific Tales (Cryptids)

The further he runs into the woods, hurdling fallen branches and breaking through bushes and clusters of trees, the deeper and more painful the realization becomes that he had just lost the only other being that ever understood him – to the fear of his brethren.

But he is alive. Maybe he will find her again.

Follow Justine's work here:

His Grandmother's Eyes

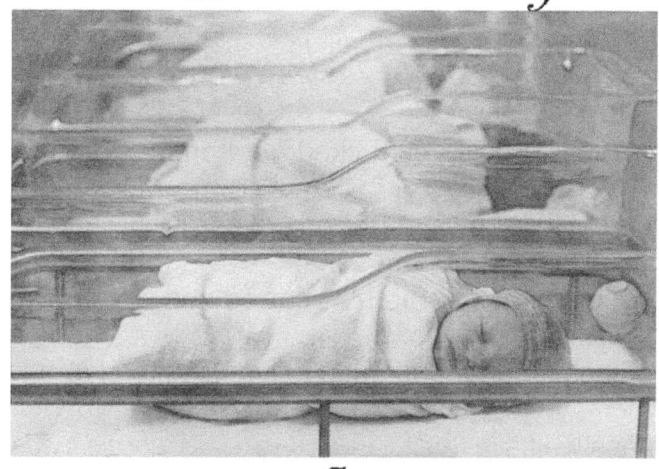

by
Bruce Buchanan

"You want me to kidnap an unborn baby?" John Thomas stroked his stubbly chin. His eyes narrowed at the tall blonde woman sitting across the table in the by-the hour motel room. *This could be a trap. Still, I'm intrigued—let's hear her out.*

Alexis Fullington tucked her hands under the leather patch elbows of her brown corduroy jacket, as if repulsed by the room's scarred and stained furnishings. John found such settings suited his business well.

John was "hired muscle" for the type of syndicate not listed on the New York Stock Exchange. But he'd kept his eyes and ears open on the streets and read every book he could check out of the prison library.

John learned that to get ahead, you had to be your own boss. So, when Alexis contacted him through his cryptic page on the Dark Web, he took the meeting. Particularly when she promised a life-changing payday.

But this job was a bit unusual, even for John. He'd never been asked to kidnap an infant before, much less one still days away from being born. His knee bounced like a piston; every sense attuned to any sign of a set-up.

Alexis found her voice again. "Well, I prefer to think of it as securing an asset. As I said, I'm part of an enterprise with vested interests. Our test results indicate this child has…unique metabolic properties that could advance our research by years. Decades, even."

John raised his eyebrows and looked around the room. The queen bed slumped in the middle, covered by a cheap, threadbare bedspread. An unpatched crack played along the wall behind the dented TV—a 1990s tube model—bolted to the nightstand. *If she came here alone without even backup, she must need this kid bad.*

"Lemme guess: Mom doesn't want to play ball, right?" He thumbed through the dossier of information he'd gathered in the days since agreeing to the meeting. The mom-to-be, 24-year-old Susan Van Manheim, lived with her own mother, Jessica Van Manheim, in the family's historic mansion in Charlotte's tony Myers Park neighborhood. Clearly, they didn't need whatever exorbitant bribe John's client offered for the child.

But Alexis obviously wasn't taking "No" for an answer. After digging into her background, John knew that she was the CEO of a biotech startup – Fullco Therapeutics. This was still a very small enterprise, hence why she had to do her own grunt work in this case. She looked away from John's knowing gaze, realizing that he knew more about her than he was letting on.

He glanced out the window as well. A stripped car stood on concrete blocks by the motel's graffiti-tagged dumpster. *Helluva place to negotiate a seven-figure deal....*

HORRORific Tales (Cryptids)

Alexis cleared her throat. "Susan…has been reluctant to cooperate. She doesn't understand the potential her child holds. He's the key to unlocking all types of mysteries about the human body. But Jessica won't let us anywhere near her daughter. I've never met anyone so…overprotective."

She turned to John. "That's why I contacted you. Our work is too important to delay. Who knows when—or if—another asset like this will come along?"

John's mouth curled into a cold smile. He wasn't a financial expert, but a simple internet search told him all he needed to know about Fullco Therapeutics. The company had burned through all its seed money and hadn't been able to raise additional venture capital. Fullco was one swirl away from going down the drain. *Which means I have Ms. Ivy League here under a barrel.*

He shrugged. "I dunno. I mean, it can be done. But I'd be the one sticking my neck out…."

Alexis sighed. Her chin dropped to the black turtleneck she wore under her blazer. "Our investors demand results, Mr. Thomas. This is the only way to deliver. I'm prepared to pay you double our original offer up front…."

Double? John would've settled for the original offer. He'd hoped he could nudge her into a ten percent increase. *But double? I'll never have to take another job.*

Closing the manilla folder, he nodded. "Ms. Fullington, I think we can do business."

***

The odor of antiseptic floor cleaner stung John's nose. He squinted under the bright fluorescent lights.

A woman behind the desk hailed John as he ambled past the nursing station that served as the maternity wards nerve center. "Orderly? Sorry—I don't know your name. There's a patient transfer on Floor Two. Can you please help?"

Under a surgical mask, John nodded and walked away from the nursing supervisor. HIPAA be damned, John had learned that Susan Van Manheim's C-section was scheduled for this afternoon. A contact on the black market hooked him up with a bogus, but functional, hospital security badge. The fresh set of scrub clothes completed the disguise.

To everyone scrambling around the bustling maternity ward, John was just another worker bee, buzzing from station to station. And then, he saw his flower. His pulse jumped, and he had to force himself to turn away. *They're here! Better not stare.*

Susan Van Manheim stepped off the elevator, gripping her mother's arm. Behind them, a burly fellow John felt sure he was a chauffeur or other hired hand lugged in the mother-to-be's bags for her stay.

Susan's hands trembled as she clutched her mother's red wool sweater. Beads of perspiration dotted her forehead as she slumped into the ward. Her basketball-shaped belly bulged from underneath her faded gray sweatshirt.

Jessica Van Manheim, on the other hand, stood ramrod straight, her eyes hidden behind dark designer sunglasses. Her brightly polished black boots clacked against the tile floor. Streaks of white highlighted her styled reddish-brown hair.

John turned away but craned his neck toward the new arrivals to overhear their conversation.

"There, there, dear. It will be over soon, and our sweet Sebastian will be here." Jessica's leather-gloved hand patted her shaking daughter's forearm.

"I know, Mom. But I'm nervous." The young woman leaned her head against her mother's shoulder.

Jessica pulled her daughter into a hallway hug. "It'll be okay. I promise."

The two women then went to the check-in desk, while John pretended to be busy.

"I'm Jessica Van Manheim, and this is my daughter, Susan. I called ahead—her private room is ready, correct?" She stood upright, hand on hip. The nurse clicked her computer's mouse and assured her that all the pre-paid arrangements were set.

Satisfied, Jessica placed both palms on Susan's slumped shoulders. "I am here for you, my dear, and I always will be. For you and Sebastian."

The back of John's neck tingled as he struggled to control his excitement. *That will be one promise you can't keep, old lady.*

With a few hours to kill until the operation, John decided to walk through his escape route one more time. *I'm leaving nothing to chance. No surprises.*

***

"He's here and he's a healthy, beautiful baby! Sebastian Van Manheim!" The OB/GYN doctor's voice carried from the operating room to the adjacent supply closet, where John had stocked and restocked the same materials a half-dozen times.

He grinned under his mask. He knew that the baby would be cleaned up and given a few minutes with his mother before going to the nursery for some standard procedures and tests.

Sure enough, within moments, a nurse wheeled the child out in a plastic bassinet lined with blue surgical towels.

John gave her an easy wave. "I've got this one, Sherry. Chrystal needs you to start an IV in Room 336." Hacking into the maternity ward's duty roster paid dividends. Sherry wasn't likely to question someone familiar with the names and assignments of her co-workers. *If she does, there are plenty of places to hide a body in a hospital. At least long enough for me to get somewhere with white sand beaches and no extradition treaties.*

The nurse put her hand to her chin. "O…okay. But I'm not supposed to release custody of the baby until I check in at the nursery."

John shook his head. "I know. It's just that word is you're the best on the floor at finding a vein, so we need you."

Sherry's face lit up. "Oh! Well, I guess it's okay this once. I mean, it is an emergency…." She took her hands off the bassinet's handle, and John steered it to the elevator.

Let's take a look at this "asset." Peeling back the swaddling blankets, John flinched. The newborn already had a full head of reddish-brown hair, just like his mother and grandmother. But John's attention quickly went to the baby's eyes. They were iridescent yellow and almost glowed—like those of a predatory animal.

Brrr! Weird-looking kid. I wonder if those eyes are related to why my client is so eager to get their hands on him?

John punched the elevator's "DOWN" button. But instead of stopping at the nursery, he directed it to the hospital's underground parking deck, where his getaway car awaited. He kept his surgical mask and tight-fitting hairnet on, knowing the hospital had security cameras everywhere.

They'll figure out who I am eventually. But I just need a few hours. Long enough to make the exchange and get out of the country.

"Heh. Buckle up, you little freak." John strapped Sebastian into the infant car seat he'd purchased for this job. *Wouldn't do to get pulled over for something dumb like a seatbelt violation.*

"WAAHHH!" Sebastian's wails escaped through the open car door and echoed off the parking deck's cavernous concrete walls.

"Shhh! Be quiet!" John looked around and when he was sure no one was looking, he dumped the empty bassinet in his car's trunk. Wouldn't do to have some do-gooder find it and call security.

HORRORific Tales (Cryptids)

John's heart raced as he closed his door and cranked the car. In minutes, they would be on the interstate heading to John's safe house Nothing stood between him and riches. If only Sebastian would stop crying….

Stupid brat. Well, he'll Alexis Fullington's problem in a couple of hours. Nothing I'll ever have to worry about again.

***

"Will you ever shut up?"

John rested his head against the safehouse's cracked, bare wall. Nothing he had done for the past two hours calmed Sebastian. The newborn wailed in the back bedroom as an exasperated John retreated to the kitchen.

Then silence. John lifted his head. *Had the kid worn himself out?* Then he swallowed hard. *What if something's wrong?* Alexis wouldn't pay his seven-figure fee if the "asset" died.

He raced to the bedroom, which was empty save for a cheap plastic green-and-blue crib John picked up at a yard sale.

He looked inside the crib, where Sebastian rested on a bare mattress. Not only was the child healthy but he grinned and giggled. The baby's yellow eyes flashed with mischief when he looked up at John.

John scratched his head. *That's strange. Why is he suddenly so happy? It's almost like he sensed something that changed his mood. But he's eight hours old. What could he possibly know?*

KNOCK! KNOCK!

His uncertainty would have to wait. He expected Alexis to arrive at any moment. Still, he pulled out his 9mm pistol and held it close to his chest as he peered through the peephole.

Sure enough, his client stood on the other side, a baseball cap pulled low over her face. Her foot tapped a staccato beat against the rotting wooden porch. John tucked the gun into his shoulder holster and unlatched the front door.

"You sure like to bring a girl into sketchy parts of town." She quickly pushed the door closed behind her and exhaled.

"Sorry. Doing a cash-only anonymous rental limits your options." John rolled his eyes. "Tell you what: Next time, we can meet over in Ballantyne. Maybe grab cosmos and hit up the spa while we're committing felonies."

"Spare me the sarcasm, Mr. Thomas." Alexis took off her cap and hung it on a peg by the door. She smoothed her long hair with her hand. "You sure this place is secure?"

"May not be the most desirable zip code, but it's private. We're on a dead-end street, the house next door is vacant, and those big oak trees you passed hide the front of the house. No one's going to find us here."

Alexis nodded. "Very well. Now let's see the asset."

John smiled and beckoned her into the single-story home's bedroom. "The little hairball is right here."

They stepped into the room. The baby cooed as he drifted in and out of a peaceful sleep. Alexis put her hand on the crib's rail and leaned over to examine Sebastian. "Don't tell me you have a magic touch with babies, Mr. Thomas."

"Fine. I won't tell you." John didn't mention the baby's sudden mood shift moments earlier. *He'll probably start crying again any second. But he's her problem now.*

John patted the front pocket of his jeans to ensure that he still had his forged passport. Then he pulled out his phone and checked his offshore account for the tenth time that day. The money still was there, just as Alexis had promised.

THUMP! John jumped at the sound of the front door opening.

Alexis dug her fingernails into his forearm. "You said no one knew we were here!" she hissed.

"I-I didn't think they did." He pulled out the pistol. His adrenaline surging, he put his back to the cracked plaster wall and inched toward the bedroom door.

John spun into the kitchen/living room area, his gun pointed straight ahead. Jessica Van Manheim stood in front of the now-closed front door, looking as out of place as a Monet in McDonald's.

The baby's grandmother folded her hands at her waist. She still wore her dark sunglasses, the wrinkles on her forehead knitted deep into ridges.

Jessica removed her glasses and John gasped. *Her eyes!* They were the same glowing, animal-like orbs that her grandson had. But John had little time to consider that—his concern was how she had found him.

His knees shook as he gawked at his visitor.

"You! How the hell did you find us?" Alexis stood beside John, hands folded across her chest.

Jessica tucked her glasses into the neck of her sweater. "I believe there has been a mistake, sir. I made it clear to Ms. Fullington that my grandson is not for sale at any price."

John grabbed her bony forearm and yanked her into the room and away from the door. His head furiously swiveled as he awaited the police and private security to flood the safehouse. But all remained quiet, save for the overhead buzz of a dying incandescent light bulb.

HORRORific Tales   (Cryptids)

"How did you find us? And who else is with you." John pointed the gun at Jessica. But her eyes strayed toward the bedroom. Sebastian giggled more loudly than John thought a newborn could.

"No one else is with me. My daughter is still recovering from her C-section and besides, the pack always takes care of our own. I figured it was better for me to come alone." She slowly padded across the bumpy linoleum floor and peeked into the bedroom.

She sighed upon seeing her grandson.

"As for how I tracked him, let's just say I have a nose for it. I think my grandson does, too. He knew his grandmother was coming." Alexis shivered visibly at those words. Her mouth dropped open.

John kept the gun trained on Jessica, but his other hand went to his chin. *If this old bat really came alone, this might be the luckiest break of my career.*

That meant Jessica Van Manheim couldn't be allowed to live. Shrugging, he tucked his gun in his shoulder holster. The shots might be too loud even out here. He'd have to do this the old-school way: strangulation.

He reached for Jessica's throat.

"No! You don't understand—"

But John ignored Alexis and continued toward his target. "Look, lady, I'm sorry about this, but—"

That's when John Thomas' right wrist shattered like porcelain under Jessica's grip.

"AIEEEH!!" His heart rate surged as he pulled his broken, useless hand to his body and backed away. *How…how did she…?*

He didn't finish the thought. Instead, a blur of rusty brown hair flashed, as Jessica closed the distance between them. Lifting him by his throat with one hand, she spiked him back-first into the wall, smashing a bowling ball-sized hole through the plaster and sheetrock.

"How dare you threaten my family!"

Jessica turned her attention to Alexis, who backed away with shaking hands and tears streaming down her face.

John gasped in quick, ragged spurts. A burning sensation ran through his chest, which John suspected meant at least one rib had broken.

Still, John bit his lower lip and pulled out his pistol again. Heat rushed to his face. The smart play would've been to run from…whatever this was. But John Thomas took pride in his profession. He couldn't allow anyone to embarrass him this way.

BANG!BANG!BANG!

The bullets sank into Jessica's back before she could reach Alexis. Her body stiffened, then crumbled to the floor. Alexis leaned against the dingy wall, her hands on her knees as she tried to pull oxygen into her lungs.

John strained his ears for any sign of others coming. He heard nothing, but every instinct told him to flee.

He kept his lone duffel bag packed and ready to go at a moment's notice in the same room as Sebastian's crib. Despite the loud rapport of gunshots, the baby continued cooing and laughing.

He stumbled into the bedroom. *Gotta…get outta here! Hole up, until I can recover.*

"Sigh….You really should've used silver bullets." Jessica's calm voice sent a chill down John's back. His grip tensed before he could lift the bag.

The prim and proper grandmother stood in the bedroom doorway. One hand perched on her hip. With the other, she deposited Alexis Fullington's lifeless body on the floor. Blood dripped from the tips of Jessica's manicured red fingernails.

With a smile, she then swept the dust off her sleeves, unaffected by the three gunshots. "TSK! This sweater is a Tory Burch and you have ruined it."

John's eyes went wide; a vein visibly pumped in his neck. Unable to make his legs work, he turned over and collapsed on the seat of his pants. *Wha— what is she?*

HORRORific Tales (Cryptids)

Jessica stepped across the room and kissed her grandson's forehead. He wriggled in his crib at his grandmother's touch. "You see, the Van Manheim family is…well, 'cursed' is the colloquial phrase. I've never thought of it in such terms. But we *are* lycanthropes. That means 'Werewolves,' you stupid, evil man."

John stammered to find words that would not come. Jessica, however, experienced no such problem. "There's only one challenging aspect to our condition. We require blood on occasion. Human blood. And while I hoped my grandson's first meal would be under better circumstances, the sweet boy is famished."

And at that, the grandmother's face sprouted thick amber fur. Her nose and mouth elongated into a snout, and her mouth filled with dagger-like fangs. Only her eyes remained unchanged. They drew closer to John.

"NO!!"

After a moment, John's screaming stopped, replaced by the gentle sound of a baby cooing.

Follow Bruce's work here:

HORRORific Tales				(Cryptids)

And at that, the grandfather's face sprouted thick amber fur. His nose and mouth elongated into a snout, and her mouth filled with dagger-like fangs. Only his eyes remained unchanged. They drew closer to John.

"NO!"

After a moment, John's screams were stopped, replaced by the gentle sound of a bone cracking.

Follow Ember's dark tales...

Husker

by
Lee Swift

HORRORific Tales   (Cryptids)

Allegheny County Jail, PA,

August 1988

"You're making my job harder" Rick said as he entered Susie's cell. His tone was the soft side of annoyed, spoken low enough to keep out of the prying ears of her neighbours.

The cell was cooler than outside, but he still felt the sweat on his body; his beige suit bearing the signs of it around the seams.

"My Son. Is he alright?"

Rick sat on the wicker chair the guards had brought in, running his hands through his dusky blonde hair, clammy from the day's heat.

"Josh's with your parents" he said, wafting his collar.

"What?"

He re-adjusted himself into the lawyer she needed him to be, and cleared his throat before answering.

"When your trial starts, your home will be a media circus - that's no place for an eight year old. Besides, your husband's busy, going on any broadcast and radio show that'll listen."

"That's good, right? Bob'll add credibility to my statement."

"Honestly? No" Rick said, pressing the clasps on his briefcase until they clacked open. "Commenting in public just highlights how outrageous this story is, and I think it'll ultimately hurt your case. Smoke?"

She took in his words before nodding, accepting the cigarette and light.

He was impressed. Most people recoiled at his bluntness like a dead fish under their nose.

"I'll be straight with you, Mrs Wallace, with the nature of your claims and how you and your husband are choosing to play it, I'm struggling to see why you accepted my council at all."

"If you can't figure that out, then maybe I *am* wasting my money" she said, leaning back into the darkness of the bunk. "I know how it sounds. I know they're pushing for a death sentence, that's why I need you…I *need* the best."

Rick drew on his own cigarette, studying her. She had a casual assurance to her, like she'd given up trying to convince anyone; wildly different from the arrest report he'd read.

"Quit staring at me like that" she said, drawing her legs to her chest.

"Like what?"

"Like I'm crazy. I'm not crazy. That *thing* down there killed Walton Bridges, not me."

"We're going to have a hell of a time proving that, especially now you're confined to your cell. You know they've taken your shoes for a reason, right?"

Susie shrugged, "I've never been good at dealing with authority, not from cops, or from bitches in prison tangerine. I'm no pushover."

He drew out a gleaming silver cassette recorder the size of a brick. "Unfortunately, that won't help your case, either. The prosecution's going to highlight your temperament, right off the bat. if I'm going to get you out of here, I need you to take me through it, from the beginning. Think you can do that?"

The bravado drained from Susie like juice sucked from a tomato. Those four simple words, "take me through it", were powerful. It gave Rick hope to see her well up. She had emotion, maybe even regret. He was on the right track.

"Alright" Susie said, drawing heaving on the cigarette, where do you want me to start?"

Rick pressed the keys on the recorder, filling the cell with the soft whirr of gears.

"Start with the boy they found."

* * *

Part 1: The National Tragedy

Morningside, PA, May 1988

Tommy Turner was on the milk cartons less than two weeks after his disappearance.

Susie didn't notice until she saw the other moms crying on the sidelines at little league.

She'd always resisted standing with the gaggle of gossips, preferring to help Josh perfect his swing. This week was different. They said Tommy had been gone for days. The mother, Mary-Beth was bed-ridden with grief.

It upset Susie enough to hear such tragedy, but that night, folding the laundry, she found one of Josh's spare little league shirts with a feint signature. It was written in marker stains on the collar. *T.Turner.* The sight of it sent the ticklish static of cortisol and adrenaline shooting through her veins.

Tommy Turner, the innocent little outfielder; the one she'd cleaned up after scraping his knee sliding to home base, held in a damp basement, crying for his mother.

That night, Susie dreamt of that knife-wielding, child molester, lifting the hemp sack off his matted little head, only to find that boy was her son.

The next day, Susie set out to find that boy.

Bob was worried, but he didn't stop her. It was one of the things she loved about him. He called her out on bullshit, but when that fire was in her belly, he was right there.

Susie became possessed. She gathered the gossips, the PTA, neighbourhood busy bodies, and anyone else that'd listen. Together, they searched the city.

Captain McTurvey of the Pittsburgh PD discouraged it, but she had an army and a righteous cause. Susie truly believed they'd find that boy, and she couldn't, wouldn't stop, until they had.

On the eighth night, Bob's gentle shake jolted her awake.

"Wh-what time is it?" she asked, switching on the bedside lamp.

"Eleven fifty five" he said, easing down onto the edge of the bed. "Shhh, don't wake Josh."

"What's wrong?"

There it was, again, that jolt of chemicals up her spine. Bob looked down, shaking his head. She placed her hand on his.

"When?" she asked, tears welling up.

"They called fifteen minutes ago. Said a homeless woman found him, out by the old yards at Millvale."

"Jesus! Fifteen minutes ago? Why didn't you wake me?"

"Quiet. Don't wake Josh, remember. I almost didn't tell you at all. You're worn out. Suuz, you need rest. Going out there won't accomplish anything. Not now."

"I have to."

"You *don't*. I woke you because I love you and out of respect for what you've done. Please, Suuz, listen and respect what I'm saying to you. There's nothing more we can do. He's gone. He's…gone."

Bob edged towards her with open arms. She broke down in them, and there they stayed for a long time.

HORRORific Tales   (Cryptids)

* * *

August 1988

"You know…" Susie said, "once they found that boy, everyone wanted to let it go. National news left town and everyone was expected to pretend like the pain had gone right away with them. Most wanted that."

"But you couldn't do that?" Rick asked, stubbing out his cigarette, exhaling the last of the smoke.

"Damn right. They might've acted like they forgot, but the pain in their eyes was there, every day, and I…blamed myself."

Rick nodded. Now they were getting somewhere. He let the silence hang for her to fill.

"I-I didn't even attend that poor boy's funeral. You know that?"

"Why?"

"Because I made a vow. It was like a puzzle that'd been ripped away before I could finish it. I thought finding him would be enough, but I realised it wouldn't be over until I found the bastard that killed him. I knew they were out there, watching and waiting. I was right, only, it wasn't *someone*...and it wouldn't stop with Tommy Turner. That's why I went to the Police."

* * *

Part 2: The Autopsy

Pittsburgh PD, June 1988

"You expect me to believe this trash?"

Susie slammed the news clipping on McTurvey's desk, leaning over like a teacher scalding a pupil.

McTurvey shrugged.

"Those are the Coroner's findings, believe it or not. Mrs Turner accepts them, so if there's nothing else..."

"Mary-Beth accepts them because she's grieving and doesn't want to face the fact she was more bothered about where the bourbon was than her son."

"You're out of line" McTurvey said.

"Am I? Zodiac, John Wayne Gacy, Texarcana, Ed Gein, Ted Bundy. You get what I'm driving at? We'll be next if you don't do something."

"Listen to me. Nothing here supports that sort of crazy claim."

"Right. I'm trying to stop it before it starts, Captain. There's too much that doesn't make sense. Your officers covered that abandoned factory two days before he was found there. You say it was an accident, but how can a little boy survive almost three weeks on his own, and end up west of the river, four miles from home, without anyone seeing him?"

"Look. There was no sign of any prints or markings to indicate anyone else was involved."

"What about the poison? You couldn't identify it. That doesn't strike you as odd?"

"Just because we couldn't identify it, doesn't mean it's unknown. We're not the CDC. That building had a lot of chemicals used in it. He drank or touched something he shouldn't have. Case closed."

"And you're going to be able to sleep at night with that? You won't even send off a sample for testing?"

McTurvey leaned back knitting his fingers together.

"We've got things called budgets, here, lady, and I'm not about to blow mine and panic a whole city, just to find out what I already know. The kid died through misadventure. That's the end of it. Besides, I've not got access anymore. Site's already sold to Bridges and Cornwall. They're building a new steel yard. It'll be good for the area, create a lot of jobs. For God's sake, go home. Let the boy rest in peace."

* * *

August 1988

"But you didn't, did you?" Rick asked.

"Actually, I did" Susie said, rubbing the tiredness out of her eye. "You got any coffee?"

"Er, just water" he said, gestured outside the cell, frowning when the guard didn't move. "Guess I don't."

HORRORific Tales (Cryptids)

He passed Susie another smoke as compensation and flipped through the notes he'd made.

"If you left, what changed your mind?"

"You mean *who*. Someone approached me. Don't ask, I won't give his name. He had morals and knew we needed to protect our kids. He showed up late one night at my door, showed us the full coroner's report."

She faltered, putting her hand to her nose.

"Sorry, I…there was a-a picture of Tommy as he'd been found. I can still see it. He was mummified. I mean sucked dry. His face was yellowed and hard, like an old popped blister. He had wounds, too. Officer- *the officer*, showed us them. They were like vampire marks, but a lot freaking bigger, like a-an ice pick had been rammed into his spine."

"If you need a minute-" Rick said reaching for the tape,

"No" Susie said, wiping her eyes. I want to continue."

Rick nodded, passing across the handkerchief from his pocket.

"He showed me the toxicology screen, too.

There was next to no fluid in Tommy's body, but what was there, was infested in poison."

"I hate to say it, but Pittsburgh PD are disputing your claim, Mrs Wallace. They showed me the coroner's report. It doesn't look like that at all."

"Sure" she laughed, drying her eyes. "They knew I had to let him take it back, before they found it missing."

"This Police officer, he could be vital in your case. If we could-"

"Absolutely not. I won't sell him out. I wont."

Rick raised his hands and slapped his thighs. This was like asking him to fly to Florida whilst the passengers were dismantling the wings.

"I admire your integrity Mrs Wallace, but I'll tell you, that's the first thing to go when you're in prison."

"I don't care. There's other ways than hanging him out to dry. They can change the paperwork, but they can't change what I found."

Rick shook his head and looked outside. Part of him wanted to walk, but as crazy as she was, there was that other sliver of him that got a rush when he heard the story. This was always going to be a challenge, why back out before knowing all the odds?

"If you've got something" he said, "let's hear it."

"Bob and I knew damn well it'd be our word against theirs, so we looked for evidence, and sure enough, we found our killer. We found the Husker."

* * *

Part 3: The Husker

August 1988

"The who?" Rick asked.

Susie shook her head, taking a long drag on the cigarette, tapping the ash into the cup of her hand.

"Uh uh, if I tell you straight out, you'll only go on believing I'm crazy. You said, yourself, you need the full story."

"Fine" Rick sighed

"After we'd seen that report, we knew what to look for. Bob and I searched press cuttings and got sea sick on the microfiche more than I care to remember. This was over, say, a month. Finally, we got two hits. A little girl in seventy six and construction worker in eighty, both found in Millvale, both were poisoned with no prints at the scene."

"That backs up Brian McTurvey's account."

"Sure" Susie said, "except these articles had more to say. The man was tearing the factory down. That floor was thick with plaster and concrete dust and still, there wasn't a single print. You understand that? It hinted at other deaths, too, but nothing else was in the news, so we went to the obituaries. That took us days. Josh isn't a reader, but his English skills went through the roof when we took him with us. By the end, we found forty deaths by misadventure in a thirty year span."

"And yet they weren't in the news."

Susie shrugged. "Right."

"Impossible. Deaths like that, they' d be noticed."

She smiled, lamentably. "Every one of those others were hobos. Vagrants. The lowest criminals. Nobody to miss them."

Rick frowned. "That's, that's just supposition on your part. I can't use any of this. Where's the link? Where's the motive."

"Exactly" Susie said, suddenly animated, shifting to the edge of the bunk. "I've been where you are, now. I needed more, something to-to make it clear. I knew there was something I was missing. That's why I decided to go."

"Where?"

"Where'd you think? Bob wouldn't let me go alone, and I knew I could be arrested, so I waited until he was at work and Josh was at school. I grabbed my bag, and I went to Millvale. I went to catch a killer."

*　*　*

Millvale, PA, July 1988

Even in daylight, the building felt sinister. The cold, summer shower only added to it.

The sign on the fence told her she'd got the right place. Medivex. The pharmaceutical company had gone bust; the site partially demolished, then left as a blight on the landscape.

Despite the fire inside her demanding action, her legs refused to pass beyond the rusted chain fence and Police tape that lay snapped and discarded in the mud. She licked her dry lips and shook her head.

"This is stupid" she whispered, "You're going to get hurt…you can't do this."

She closed her eyes, repeating the words, then blew a short, sharp, breath and lifted the snipped fence.

As casual as she could manage, Susie hurried across the rain-slick concrete towards the old block, ignoring the rattling fence as it settled.

The brickwork was still intact, interspersed with dark gaping holes, all along the second floor. The rain made it impossible to be sure nobody was watching her from behind their jagged teeth of glass.

Clutching her hood and lowering her head, she making her way around the building.

Outlines of older facilities scarred the landscape, artworks of graffiti adorning their ruinous brick. Among them, a white arrow sprayed on the ground pointed to chipboard panels covering part of the factory wall. The board was soaked and rotten. Nails had been prized out enough to allow it to bend it outwards, leaving enough space to slide through.

Susie gagged as she entered. Inside reeked of piss and mould. The walls were desecrated much like the exterior. Rusted bed springs lay on ashen remains of fires, ragged bedclothes, and the odd needle were piled in the corners, away from the dripping gaps in the roof. Then there were the cobwebs. They were small at first, growing thicker the further she ventured from the main hall.

She stopped at one of the offshoot corridors, peering down the stairs, through the thick coating of webs, to the lower level.

On the lip of the low ceiling, thick stylised letters marked a phrase, bold enough to stand out from the rest of the thousand scrawls, another arrow, pointed downwards to the black corridor.

Husker.

The sudden tap on her shoulder made her gasp with shock.

The man she saw recoiled in shock. His beard was patchy and like old wire. His sunken eyes watched her nervously as he adjusted his deer stalker hat, an odd choice, given the season. He blinked profusely, holding out his grubby, nicotine stained hands which were covered with fingerless gloves.

"Who are you?" Susie asked, still gasping from the surprise.

"Sh-Shouldn't be here."

"No shit!" she said. "Who are you?"

"...Jim. Don't hang around here. It's not safe."

"Why?"

He nodded to the corridor "It'll hear you."

"What the hell are you talking about?"

"Came about the boy, right?" he asked, lowering his hands, slowly.

"I'm here about a lot of people" Susie said, following him uneasy, back towards the main hall.

"Not a cop, then."

"Why'd you say that?"

"Cops don't care. One of us goes missing, one less to beat."

"Did you see what happened to that little boy?"

He bit at his fingernails, eyeing her with suspicion.

Susie fished out a twenty from her purse. "Tell me what you know. I need proof."

Jim shrugged, taking the note, hesitating when she kept hold, forcing him to meet her gaze.

"*Proof*" she emphasised.

He nodded, earnestly, and beckoned her away.

"What is that? Palm tree bark?"

What Jim held was tubular, crisp like old paper and ragged at the edges. Hundreds of thin ochre fibres protruded from its surface.

"It's proof" Jim said. "Deon, my buddy, found it. He's dead now, so it's mine."

"Where'd he find it?"

"Down there, where it lives."

"*It*? What're you saying?"

"You've seen the webs. That's all any of us see, but we find bodies. Sometimes long after. Deon was braver than us. Went down, found it, and barely got out. This ain't palm bark, lady, this is its skin."

Susie sat on the ground, ignoring the pool of rainwater dripping in from the leaks above, eyes darting with horrified contemplation.

"All of those deaths, the homeless…why?"

"Birds gotta fly, fish gotta swim. Husker's no different. It eats."

"No, why'd you stay?"

Jim shrugged, easing the skin back into it's hiding place.

"Nowhere to go. Outside, you get busted, go to jail, end up someone's bitch or shanked. Take your chances, here, you can get your hit. Cops don't come around. Nobody bothers nobody. Husker feeds once a while, does the job for them. They pimp their city to tourists. Everyone's happy. Especially Husker."

* * *

Part 4: Hunter and Prey

August 1988

The tape clacked to a stop.

Rick cupped his hands around his mouth, gathering his thoughts.

"You want me to present evidence from a heroin addict who claims a giant spider's eating his friends. That it killed Walton Bridges, Tommy Turner, and thirty nine others?"

"I'm. Not. Crazy" Susie said. "That site was a chemical plant that had indirect links to the US Govenrment. McTurvey admitted as much. Who knows what leaked into the environment, or what they experimented with?"

"Say it's gospel, why's nobody seen this Husker? People would've come forward."

"Bob looked into that place afterwards. He said it was built on top of a civil war munitions factory. There's corridors and storage bunkers beneath it, running both sides of the river."

"That's where the cops found you when they took you in, right?"

"Yeah, but that's not all. After I was arrested, Bob asked the kids at little league about it. They call it the ghost passage. Tommy went there with his friends, but they were too scared to go in. Don't you get it? Tommy entered those tunnels and didn't come back. It's lived there for decades. Jim was right. People did see it, but they were hushed up for the sake of the tourist economy and to stop panic. That's why McTurvey was cagey when I pushed him about the autopsy. That's why they came for me when they saw I'd gone into that site."

HORRORific Tales (Cryptids)

* * *

Millvale, PA, July 1988

Susie piqued her ears as the car door slammed.

She shushed Jim as voices gradually drifted into earshot.

"-seen her come in. Lyle's gone round the other way."

"What?" Jim asked.

She didn't dare speak. The options raced in her mind. She could give up. This wasn't her world, she could go back to her suburbia and live in ignorant bliss, just like McTurvey wanted her to.

She grabbed Jim's arm as the boards moved, bolting towards the stairwell, brushing aside the blanket of webs as she went.

Jim tore his arm away once he realised their destination.

"Y-You're crazy!" he said. "Don't go there!"

"They'll find us!" she countered.

A yell came from the main room. Jim's eyes grew wide. He skipped a step, then broke into a run.

Drumming of boots against the wet concrete followed an instant later.

Susie raced down the steps, wheeling into a darkened passage some way inside. There she paused, clutching the decayed timber supports. She wouldn't go on, unless she had to.

Flashlights bounced off the steps she'd run down, sliced in two by the low lip of the ceiling.

"Here. Footprints. Let's go."

The voice was masculine and southern.

One by one, three other voices, more native to Pittsburgh, announced their reluctance.

"What you say?"

"No disrespect, Mr Bridges, but there's, ah, rumours about this place."

"You shitting me? You're scared of a rumour?"

"They ain't just rumours" the third man said. "If she's gone in there, then God help her."

The words sent a chill through her. The tingle, already plaguing her neck, intensified.

"We should go tell McTurvey."

"Leave?" the first voice asked. "You simple sons of bitches might be happy to let this here woman go, but I've got millions invested in this goddamned place. I intend to find her and expose her lies in a court of law. Now, as officers of the law, y'all telling me you won't help?"

Susie shivered in the silence, breath baited.

Bridges growled; one of the beams dancing sporadically as he snatched a flashlight.

"Go on then, get. I'll do my civic duty and y'all can just hand your badges in when it's done."

She eased back into the darkness the second she heard his feet on the stairs, the torchlight narrowly missing her as she dodged into another opening.

Tracking her was easy for Bridges, her footprints clear in the centuries of dust. She abandoned any sense of stealth, running headlong into the darkness. She tripped and stumbled through the maze, gulping in the warm, musty air. tearing through thick swathes of cobwebs, each stickier than molasses, more resilient than the last. They were all encompassing, suffocating to the point where the feel of their silken strands roused up a panic inside her. She wanted to scream, tear and run until she was free of it all. Bridges' curses from the corridor behind her said he was feeling it too.

"Goddamn it! Come back here!"

Bridges puffing and gasping told her she was in better shape; she had a reprieve. But how long?

She slowed, orienting herself away from the shouts, punching through the tough strands of web and scraping along the old dirt walled surface until she bumped into something raised from it. Parts flaked in her hand, but was solid; rising parallel with the wall. She found another, and a joining piece between them.

A ladder? An old, rusted ladder.

Scattered light, pierced the webs, casting a ghostly afterglow into the room she was in, highlighting the lip of the next level

Susie gasped and hauled herself up, feet furiously clattering against rusted bars as Bridges entered.

"Got ya!" He roared.

HORRORific Tales (Cryptids)

Susie leaped, bringing her upper body over the lip, screaming with all the breath left within her, as the torchlight illuminated the monster, crouched low by the ladder, ready to pounce.

Its face was twice as wide as hers. It's fangs, bright as ivory, glinted in the growing light. Where there were once eyes, there were now ragged holes, showing the burgundy interior of the sockets.

Instinctively, Susie recoiled, slipping on the ladder with a clang, smashing her knee against the rung. Every sense in her recoiled from that thing, despite the sound of Walton Bridges crossing the room, but the split second before she did, she caught sight of the shreds of skin that had erupted outwards from the sternum, their folds now motionless, hardened and withered flaps of skin. She gasped, as she noticed one of it's many legs, each one as tall as an adult male, was snapped and stunted.

A hand clamped onto her ankle like a wolf's jaw, forcing a fresh scream from her and an immediate back-heel kick.

"G-get down here you trespassin' little bitch!"

She grabbed the ladder, using it for leverage, stamping and kicking until she heard him howl in pain and a clatter.

Susie vaulted up the final three rungs to the top, collapsing into the dirt, in front of the husk.

A sliver of daylight shone through a fissure in the cracked wall, giving just enough light to pick out the edges of the uneven, natural formed walls. They'd crumbled over time. It'd be a squeeze, but she'd get through.

"You don't know what you're doing!" Bridges yelled, the rungs vibrating as he put his weight upon them. "Let's talk!"

"Fuck you!" Susie screamed.

Suddenly, the cave lost it's glow as she scrambled to her feet; a deep seated dread burst from the core of her soul.

Something moved. It was as quiet as a panther as it's bulk slipping over the sliver of the opening, plunging the room into darkness.

Susie tripped backwards, the giant husk's desiccated leg crunching under her weight.

Torchlight returned from the room below, catching the edges of the room.

HORRORific Tales   (Cryptids)

She saw it and wished to everything holy that she didn't. She wanted to curse it for the murders, denounce it, but her words dried like the spittle in her mouth, reduced to terrified whimpers of insanity.

It moved like night itself, silent, slow and horrifying, like undead fingers emerging from the confines of a coffin.

If Walton Bridges hadn't crested the ladder, cursing and shouting as he went, maybe Susie would have been the victim, sucked dry by the mandibles that chattered and clacked like a rattlesnake as the light from Walton's flashlight shone upon them.

The Husker pounced, steel-like tendons launching it forwards, Susie felt the wind against her face as it passed over her.

As the flashlight clattered down the rungs, it's afterglow hinting at the powerful gigantic legs, pinning Bridges to the ladder, fangs puncturing his cranium. Muffed screams emerged from the folds of horrendous black skin that enveloped Walton Bridges' head, all part of the monster's maw.

* * *

August 24th 1988

Rick sat for a good minute. He took out his cigarette, lighting it before he realised he'd only half smoked the last one.

Susie waited patiently.

"Ah...um, so how did you get out?"

She licked her lips, contemplating the answer. Tears were near her eyes.

"I waited. I didn't dare move incase it noticed me. Maybe it'd had it's fill, I don't know, but it eventually dragged his body up the wall. He was dead by then, limp. I took the chance, raced down the ladder and out."

"Police found you near those steps, covered in cobwebs and Mr Bridges' blood, right?"

Susie nodded.

Rick rocked to his feet.

"Wait, that's it?"

"Mrs Wallace" Rick said, exhaling the smoke, "I like a challenge. What you've given me, is a herculean ordeal. I was hoping for something I could get reasonable doubt on, but by your own words, you're the last to see the victim. You had his blood on you."

"I don't care what it looks like" Susie said, "If you don't help me, how long before another Tommy Turner shows up?"

Rick clacked open his briefcase and slipped the recorder inside.

"You heard of Bigfoot, Mrs Wallace?"

"Yeah."

"Well, I can't convince a jury to believe in your Bigfoot sighting, and the land's sold, so I can't go in those tunnels and get the evidence you want. What I *can* do, is promise I'll fight to prove Medivex didn't clear the site properly, and the victims were exposed to violent, corrosive and harmful chemicals. I'll do my level best to expose the fact that Pittsburgh PD covered up the number of deaths from these chemicals to keep tourism flowing and legal battles about shit leaking into the water system off the table. I'll even work on a plea bargain, get your sentence reduced to trespassing."

He eased himself onto the bunk beside her.

"I've defended the worst pieces of human trash the world has to offer, and I've done it for fifteen years. In that time, I've learned that sometimes, there's doors you just don't open; questions you can live your whole life without answering. In time, you'll get your life back, and when you do, for the sake of your family, I'm advising you, forget the *Husker.* You said it's been here thirty years and there's been no outcry, I see no reason why that wouldn't be the case, now. Let it go. Focus on your son and your husband, alright?"

Susie nodded "...Alright. Alright, I promise."

Rick sighed, glancing back with disappointment as he stepped into the sun-baked corridor of the prison.

He knew a lie when he heard it.

Check out Lee's work here:

HORRORific Tales (Cryptids)

La LeChuza

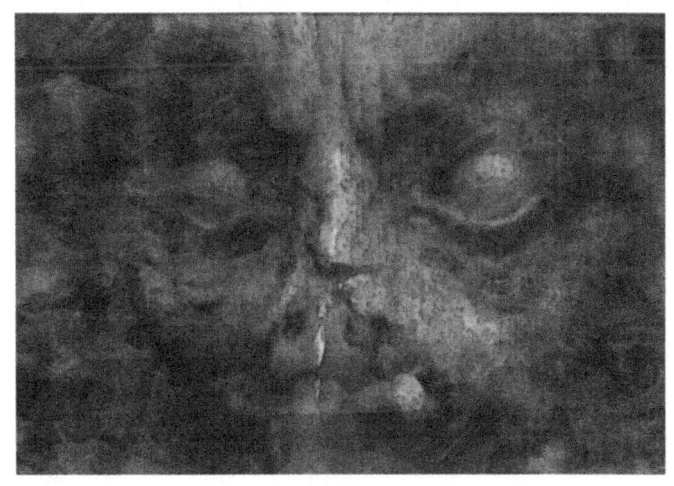

by
Gene Baker

HORRORific Tales (Cryptids)

New Spain Viceroyalty

July 1786

Seeking relief from the fiery rays of the noontime sun, Captain Leon Alvarez of the Spanish Imperial Guard stood in the shade of an ancient oak tree in the Presidio's courtyard. For a moment, he imagined himself instead in the flower-scented gardens of his native Castile. Then the oppressive humidity and the unceasing buzz of flies brought him back to the reality of his situation. He hated being in this colonial shit-hole. For now, however, he had no choice.

The Governor tapped his glass against the bottle he was holding and asked, "Some more wine Capitán?"

As much as Alvarez disliked this part of the King's possessions, he absolutely despised the short, fat, sorry excuse for a man addressing him. "I would rather drink my horse's piss." He growled in return.

The Governor dropped his half-hearted smile into a full, angry scowl and groused, "No need to be rude, Capitán, you…"

"Let me see if I understand what has occurred here." The Castilian interrupted.

"Your idiot son forced himself on one of these half-native, Negrito bitches. She became pregnant so you sent your men to kill her and her child to protect whatever you consider your family's honor.

"This, without regard for the truth that those French bastards across the river would use the incident to stir up the natives and force us to fight them in front of us and the Mexicano rebels behind us.

"There is also the drumming and chanting I heard on my way here coming from where I was told, the woman and her maggot were killed.

"All of this makes a Devil of a mess my soldiers are charged with cleaning up!"

Desperately trying to regain the upper hand, the Governor snapped back, "The King himself will be made aware of your insubordination!"

Leon Alvarez sneered at the threat and snarked in return, "I will be more than happy to deliver your message myself."

The following day, a few hours after the Captain and his men entered the forested maze on their mission, the thrumming of the ceremonial sounds ceased and the gut-wrenching screaming began.

HORRORific Tales   (Cryptids)

October 2016

Sheriff Josiah Caldwell should have been in his bed sound asleep at one in the morning but that wasn't happening. If he had gotten a total of six hours of "Rest" in the last seventy-two, it would have surprised him. The events of the past few days precluded any deep REM-Stage type of slumber.

It had been over five years since anyone had died by anything other than natural causes or a farm-related accident in this little corner of Texas. The events following the direct hit of a massive Hurricane had upset everybody's apple cart. These kinds of storms that arrive late in the season are always the worst and this one was not any different. That was the night that the eighty-year-old levee gave way from the ravaging stormwaters and washed through a large swath of the surrounding woodlands.

When the weather finally broke, the County Manager sent out a couple of dozier workers to clear away the debris on an access road to the nearby oil and gas platforms. The sun had set without their supervisor hearing back from the men, so Caldwell sent a Deputy to the area to try and make contact with them. What the woman encountered would haunt her nightmares for the rest of her life.

Anything that was left uneaten by what appeared to be feral hogs of Lucho Ocegueda was impaled on a broken-off branch high in a nearby oak. His face was forever twisted in a silent, horrified scream. His brother Miguel was lying unconscious in the muddy hole created by a giant washed-up Camphor Tree, covered in deep gashes and smelling like the putrefaction of a long-dead body.

Ever since then, the Sheriff had spent most of his restless hours either in his office or, like tonight, walking the darkened streets of the small oilfield town of Birchfield. He was letting his mind tick off every step that had been taken in the investigation for the umpteenth time when he saw the light was still on in Andy's Garage.

Entering the open bay, he began running his fingers down the scratches on the hood of Ocegueda's truck. Caldwell thinks to himself, *"They look like claw marks sure enough, but they are too deep. Animal claws would have at the most, just scuffed the paint. These went through the paint and creased the metal underneath."*

The Sheriff was concentrating so deeply on all the theories running through his sleep-deprived head, that he was startled and jumped back as his hand automatically went to his holster when he heard Joaquín Pineda mumble, "I knew I would find you here looking at those claw marks."

HORRORific Tales   (Cryptids)

The elderly farmer stood with his granddaughter, Camila, at the edge of where the flickering neon light of the "Closed" business sign cut into night's darkness. "Cammy" as she was called, looked much younger than her twenty years of age. She had a reputation among her community of being a "Curandera" or healer who had successfully recovered deathly ill people "Modern Medicine" had given up on.

Letting his burst of "Fight or Flight" subside, Caldwell released his fingers from his firearm's grip and spoke haltingly, "I'm thinking that the boys ran through some barbed wire somewhere and That is what made those scratches."

As he watches a huge grin cross Joaquín's face, the sheriff asks dismissively, "What ya' need folks?"

"We have a favor to ask of you, Sheriff."

Without looking up from where she watched her toes flick bits of gravel onto the cement floor of the garage, Camila quietly spoke in a childlike voice, "You have always been good to our people, Sheriff, and we appreciate it. That is why the Ocegueda family asked us to come to you with this request."

"Really? What would that be, Miss Cammy?"

"We need you to go with us to Miguel's hospital room. They wouldn't let us in otherwise."

***

It would be nearly four o'clock in the morning before Doctor Jovanovic could arrive to personally give the trio permission to enter his patient's room. While they waited at the Nurse's Station, Camila nervously briefed the Sheriff on what she believed the situation was.

"As the story goes, her name was Sofía, and right there in those woods near where you found the brothers, was her house. It was little more than a hut really. She lived there with her newborn son. Not only was the baby the product of rape, but he was also terribly deformed.

"No one wanted them, especially the baby's father who was the son of the Governor. So, to remove them, and any claim Sofía might have to any of the wealthy man's estate, she was accused of witchcraft and that she had laid with Satan.

"Sofía was dragged from her home and forced to watch while the house was burned to the ground with her baby, screaming in his crib inside.

"After that, the woman was taken away and garroted. Then, her body was thrown into a shallow depression, and a pile of stones was placed on top. Years later, to silence the animal-like screeching that would sometimes echo through those woods, a Camphor Tree was planted beside the makeshift grave."

"Why a Camphor?" Caldwell asked before a wide yawn could interrupt his query.

"As garlic is supposed to be for the legend of the Vampire, Camphor is for witches. When the flood uprooted the tree, taking the rocks over her with it, Sofía was released from her burial prison and will be reborn as an extremely powerful and dangerous La LeChuza or roughly translated as an 'Owl Witch' in English."

As Caldwell's eyes went wide with disbelief he said quietly, "Are you yankin' my chain, Miss Cammy just because it's gonna be Halloween in a week or so? That's a pretty far-fetched story you're asking me to risk losing my badge over!" Noting the look of absolute seriousness that the woman was giving him, the law enforcer decided to give her the benefit of a doubt and brought his challenging tone down a bit. "What does that have to do with Miguel?"

"After all those years in the ground, there wasn't much left of her physical form so she entered Miguel to regrow a new body. She will also have his mind and memories so she won't be two hundred and fifty years out of place for long. That is why time is of the essence here, and any delay could be disastrous for us all, but especially the children she will take away."

"Holy Shit!" Caldwell exclaimed. Then noticing that everyone at the station was glaring at them in disapproval, he moved in closer to Cammy and in a hushed tone asked, "She takes kids?"

"Yes. They are her preferred meal."

"So...How badly screwed are we?"

Camila closed her eyes, lowered her head, and let out a pained sigh.

"That bad huh?"

With his incredulity temporarily set aside and no other answers forthcoming, the Sheriff turned, again put his hand on his holstered sidearm, and started walking down the hall. "To Hell with permission! We're going in!"

Joaquín reached out quickly and as he gently grasped Caldwell's arm says, "A word of warning, my friend. If you pull your pistol and shoot at her, the bullet will come right back at you and leave La LeChuza unharmed."

With only a moment's hesitation, the Sheriff grumbles, "I'll try to remember that."

As he approached the hospital room, Caldwell saw Deputy Hawkins slumped over in his chair. "Hawkins! I posted you here to keep an eye on things, not to grab some Z's!"

HORRORific Tales   (Cryptids)

With all of the suddenness of a sledgehammer's fall, the lights flickered, and Miguels' cardiac monitor alarm echoed down the hallway with an incredibly loud beeping. At the same time as an ear-piercing scream of unimaginable pain and anguish exploded in the trios' ears, Deputy Hawkins fell to the floor dead, dislodging a large, pitch-black scorpion out of his mouth.

"We're too late!" Camila shouted above the din while she removed one of her sandals and smashed the arachnid as it skittered across the floor.

The locked door came off its hinges as both Joaquín and the Sheriff simultaneously hit it with their shoulders. The deafening noise went abruptly into sickening silence as the heart-stopping sight of Miguel, torn wide open from chin to the navel, shocked them into immobility. Their barely believing eyes followed the trail of blood, bone, and tissue that was smeared from the bed and out the open window.

***

As soon as Thomas Porter heard on his work radio that a crazed ritual killer was on the loose, he didn't even bother changing out of his oil and tar-covered overalls to race home. His wife, Crystal, and their newborn son would need to be safely secured in the small but solid house that he had built with his own hands for his growing family. His phone calls to Crystal, having gone unanswered, only added to the urgency of his situation.

So, before turning off of the paved highway onto the gravel road that led to his home, he called his friends at the Sheriff's Office. As soon as Caldwell was awakened from his nightmare-riddled "Nap" by the panicked voice shouting at the dispatcher, he intervened. "What's going on Tom?"

"I've tried getting a hold of Crystal about that killer being on the loose and all I get is a noise like some kind of electrical interference."

The Sheriff looks over at Camila who instantly responds, "That's her!"

"Tom!" Caldwell barked the command. "If you see anybody out there you don't recognize, Do Not Engage! I repeat, Do Not Engage! We are on our way."

***

Josiah Caldwell had known Tom Porter and Crystal Clayton all of their lives. He stood in for the girl's father at her wedding only a month after being a Pallbearer at Buck Clayton's funeral. It would now virtually tear his heart out to have to tell that sweet girl that her husband and the father of their one-month-old child had been murdered.

"He wrecked his truck." Is what he determined he would tell her as soon as he had the chance. She didn't have to know any further details. Such as, they had found Tom in his truck after it crashed through a fence and one of the posts had gone through the windshield and impaled him. And especially nothing about what Camila had determined came from an Owl, a feather that had been left like a "Calling Card", in Tom's hand.

As her friend choked with hesitation, Camila spoke up, "Has there been anyone around here that you haven't seen before?"

"Yeah," Crystal responded. "It's crazy but, just before y'all got here I thought I saw a naked woman with long, black hair standing out there at the edge of those woods."

"Where did she go?" Caldwell barked now back in "Sheriff" mode.

"I don't know. I looked to see who was coming up the road and when I looked back, she was gone.

What's going on?"

As her grandfather and the Sheriff went to investigate where Crystal had pointed, Cammy took the woman by the arm and said sternly, "Let's talk inside."

While the two stood on the threshold, Crystal turned to look back at the men who were examining something on a Yaupon bush. That is when Camila saw the blood clots in the hair on the back of the woman's head and serum oozing from a partially scabbed-over puncture wound.

With one fluid movement, the Curandera spun around, threw a handful of salt and iron filings from her medicine bag into Sofía's face, and dove to catch the baby that was falling from the monster's grasp.

As if she had been doused in scalding water, Sofía screamed in pain from her sizzling flesh and with supernatural speed leapt through a nearby window.

The Sheriff, hearing the inhuman caterwauling, turns to pursue the fiendish monstrosity that was rapidly blending into the nearby underbrush when Joaquín again interfered with his run by nearly tackling him. "Stop Josiah!" He shouted, "Those woods are Her domain now! She is hungry and wounded which is bad enough. It is also nearly nightfall and as powerful as La Lechuza is in the day, she will be nearly unstoppable then."

HORRORific Tales   (Cryptids)

***

"It looks more like some kind of claw or talon than a thorn.", The sheriff whispered more or less to himself as he used his pocket knife to flip over the object on the table that had been removed from Crystal's scalp.

As Cammy applied a thick and pungent salve to the unconscious woman's wound, she responded semi-sarcastically, "That is the reason we call the plant that it comes from 'Witches Claw'. La Lechuza stuck it in her head and used it to control her."

A sudden increase in Joaquín's snoring seemed to be the sleeping man's ten cents worth of opinion on the matter. Josiah leaned over to see for certain that there was no danger that the shotgun loaded with alternating shells of buckshot and rock salt the man cradled in his arms would accidentally discharge.

An autumn cold snap had settled in over the area after the storm had passed on through so Joaquín had lit the gas stove to remove some of the house's chill. Camila reached over, carefully picked up the still bloody thorn, and tossed it into one of the flaming burners. It sputtered resinous sparks into the air before completely catching fire and shrinking into a glowing red lump.

After Cammy reset herself next to her patient, Caldwell stretched widely before asking from the edge of near-total physical and mental exhaustion, "Is Crystal going to be okay?"

"The next few hours should tell us."

The sheriff grunted painfully as he stood. "I need to move around and get some fresh air. All that coffee has done is make me hafta piss every five minutes."

With a voice showing deep reservation, the Curandera asked, "You're not thinking of going outside, are you?"

"That is generally where the fresh air is. Besides, you yourself said there wasn't much of a chance of the bitch coming back here."

"It is only a coupla hours until dawn. But if you insist on taking that chance, be careful anyway and stay on this side of that salt boundary we set around the house."

"Sure enough."

As the Sheriff's hand reached over to grasp the doorknob he took a precautionary glance through the window. There at the top of a tree, silhouetted against a strangely bright moon, was an owl-shaped figure. "Why do they call her an "Owl Witch"? He quietly asked Camila.

HORRORific Tales (Cryptids)

"In Europe, the legends say that she is a Shape Shifter that most often takes on that form when hunting. The Indigenous People in this area in Pre-Spanish Colonial times believed that the actual bird itself can become a 'Familiar' and everything the animal sees and experiences, she does as well. Kinda like the black cat is for Anglo witches."

As the Chief Law Enforcer, it was Josiah Caldwell's job to keep the people of the county safe. That being the case, he felt that he was doing a piss-poor job of it. His friends and neighbors were dying horrific deaths and he seemed to be helpless about it. He looked up again and saw the bird's head do an almost 180-degree turn and lock its luminous eyes on him. He considered for a second about giving the thing a blast of rock salt but then thought angrily to himself, *"I'm sick and tired of this shit! It needs to end!"* Looking back at Cammy who was wiping the greasy concoction off of her hands onto an old towel, he then turned to see the glowing thorn/ember wink out. That gave him a grim idea. *"Then again, maybe I can use Sofía's feathered friend out there to my advantage."*

***

As the Sheriff picked his way carefully down the animal trails toward his destination, he would occasionally take a sideways glance around himself to make sure that the glowing amber eyes of the witch's spy still tracked him. He knew these woods and swamps like the back of his hand because, ever since he was old enough to tote a gun, he and his father would hunt in them. One suddenly important memory had brought him to stand in this very spot.

"When they came across a patch of land approximately fifty feet in diameter that reeked of petroleum distillates, Royce Caldwell pointed his hand at the valve station in the middle of the sludge pit. With an angry snort, he said, 'Drip Gas'. It is an oily liquid that condenses along the inside of pipes that, at one time, carried natural gas. Occasionally it finds a hole rusted through the casing and seeps out. And with all these dead trees, and the oil-soaked ground around here, this place would go up like an atom bomb. No open flames around here!"

"Got it, Dad!" Said twelve-year-old Josiah.

Looking at the Squirrel Rifle slung over the boys' shoulder, the father added, "No discharging of firearms either."

HORRORific Tales   (Cryptids)

As the starlit sky of the night made way for the red/ocher horizon of dawn, the usual sounds of the deep woods insects, birds, and other fauna abruptly ceased and brought the Sheriff out of his recollected childhood memories. It was as if Nature herself had thrown a blanket of fearful silence over the surrounding forest. A shiver went quickly up his spine that had nothing to do with the dusting of frost that had settled around him. When Caldwell senses more than actually hears the evil that moved among the shrubs that decades of petrol exposure had skeletonized he mumbles to himself, "Showtime!"

Spinning quickly around, Caldwell placed the sights of his pistol square center mass of the walking nightmare that stopped her approach in mid stride. Only the eyes and top of her head indicated a human woman. The lower part of the creature's face was a gore-covered raptor's beak. A feathered right arm ended in large and curved claws that held the flayed torso of a man Josiah recognized as "Big Joe Fernley". A slightly distended belly indicated that the farmer had unfortunately been the satiation of her hunger. An enormous black hog with eight-inch tusks and eyes glowing like fire stood on the left side of La LeChuza.

"Yeah. I know you're bullet-proof, but are you also fire-proof?" Snarled the Sheriff who subtly shifted his weapon to the old valve station just to the left of and behind Sofía. A well-placed burst from the auto .45 shatters the metal pipes. A split second later, a white-hot tidal wave of flame and shrapnel rips through La

Lechuza and her angrily snorting escort as the shockwave lifts Josiah Caldwell up and throws him back several feet from where he had stood.

***

Rituals. Probably nearly as ancient but with far less significant meaning as the ones performed in places of worship, were pretty much all that was left to Josiah Caldwell these days. His deceased wife Sueanne would call them "Habits" with the added description of "Nasty" attached in front of them. Like this cigarette that he lit every morning and deeply inhaled the smoke from before swinging his pain-filled legs to the floor.

Pain, physical as well as mental, slowed everything for him for the last several months. Even the next part of his daily observances, as in the brewing of a pot of the thick "Starter Fluid" that was his coffee.

Doctor Jovanovic, after vociferously declaring that, "It was nothing less than a miracle!" That his patient was still alive, had prescribed an opioid for the discomfort but Caldwell refused to take the manmade pharmaceutical. Especially since Camila's non-addictive natural medications seemed to work better with fewer side effects.

HORRORific Tales   (Cryptids)

With that thought entering his mind, he looked at the calendar on the front of his refrigerator and realized it was Wednesday and Cammy would be coming by soon for her weekly visit. Every day it seemed that Caldwell remembered a little more detail of the incident with La Lechuza back in October. He especially looked forward to this visit and telling his friend about the latest revelation. In particular, why he hadn't been turned to ashes right along with **La LeChuza**. Why he had only come away with a few broken bones and what the elderly physician had described as the equivalent of a bad sunburn. Not to mention, the part about when he was found by firefighters, he was not far from an old, broken-down truck that had been mostly turned into a melted pile of slag by the heat.

As of a few days ago and confirmed by last night's dreams, he had come to know the answer. As wild and unlikely as it seemed, Sofía, the "Real" one had, somehow, shielded him from the worst of the conflagration. The entity that had ridden the tormented and murdered woman's anger, suffering, and hatred straight out of Hell and into this world had been the true enemy. Josiah, together with the storm, had brought about the circumstances that allowed Sofía's redemption and spiritual reunion with her tiny son moments before they both stepped away into "The Light".

Caldwell's self-absorption was then gently interrupted by Cammy's soft tapping at his door. He took in a deep breath and let it back out with a whispered, "Showtime!"

Check out Gene's work here:

HORRORific Tales   (Cryptids)

Where Lava Flows

by
Demi Michelle Schwartz

HORRORific Tales   (Cryptids)

Tonight, I'll either be granted freedom, or die.

The sun sets on el Solsticio de Sacrificio as I approach Monte Cherufe alongside the other six maidens. Our white gowns billow around us in the summer breeze. My bare feet sink into black soil with each unsteady step. The Andes radiate a rosy hue in the alpenglow, and the brilliant sky drapes over my head like a canvas painted crimson, orange, and gold. Such beauty shouldn't exist on an evening like this. I try to swallow, but my throat has swollen shut.

The other members of my tribe, the Lavasores, wear robes in every color but white and stand in motionless lines on either side of the path leading to the valley, like this is a funeral procession. In a way, that's exactly what it is, but there's no casket. Why would there be? The Lavasores won't have a body to bury, since one of us will be cast into the mouth of the volcano. Only the sacrifice of a young maiden can satisfy Cherufe, the reptilian monster that dwells in the magma pool. Otherwise, my homeland would crumble from catastrophic eruptions and earthquakes.

A sob shatters the silence beside me. Blinking back tears, I reach for Katalina's hand. My little sister shouldn't be enduring such horror. I yearn for our childhood days, before we got thrust into a deadly game of chance like the other teenage girls in our tribe. Only four years ago, at thirteen, I walked this path for the first time. I've survived to my fifth and last, thanks to pure luck. I pray to Diosavola that Katalina does the same.

"Mailyn."

The choked whisper of my name drifts to me in the wind. My heart aches, as though Cherufe has sunk his fangs into my chest.

Silvio.

My love reaches for me as I pass by him, his forest-green eyes flooded with tears that reflect the setting sun. My fingers brush his for the briefest of moments. I want to promise him I'll survive, that tonight, we can fully be together for the first time, but I don't. Only Cherufe knows what's written in the stars. Do I dare hope he won't choose me? Maybe I'm not desirable enough for the monster. If so, that's fine by me. The only one I want to belong to is Silvio.

HORRORific Tales   (Cryptids)

The lines of Lavasores trickle out at the top of the steep slope. I clasp Katalina's hand tighter as we take careful steps down the hill. Black rocks tumble in an endless cascade, and their clattering echoes through the valley.

My heart pounds a syncopated rhythm. Katalina and I will survive. I must believe that. My hope can't die. Not now. Not ever.

"Mailyn," Katalina cries. "I want to go back. Please take me back."

"I can't. I'm so sorry. If I could, I would."

Tears trace rivers down my cheeks. I've never hated the monster or this ancient tradition more than I do now. Ever since we were young, Katalina has trusted me to keep her safe, and tonight, I have no choice but to drag her to her possible death.

Far below, magma flows in the deep trench surrounding the volcano. The ring of fiery liquid forming the boundary between the Lavasores' land and Cherufe's territory is the only color in the blackened landscape. Two years ago, young children dared each other to jump over the trench, and before they could return to the safe side, Cherufe emerged from the volcano and swallowed them whole. Bile churns in my stomach. I've never ventured into the monster's domain, and I hope neither Katalina nor I are forced to do so tonight.

We finish our descent and join the other maidens in front of Chief Raul. His long, gray beard and aqua robes flutter in the wind, and he holds the ceremonial basin crafted from obsidian. Sweat drips down my neck. One more time. I only need to survive one more time.

Katalina lets out a gut-wrenching cry. My heart gallops in my chest, like it's racing to get in as many beats as possible if I'm about to be sacrificed. My sister shouldn't be here. None of us should be here, but we have no choice. Girls like us have died for centuries. This vicious cycle will never end, as long as Cherufe lives.

"Line up," Chief Raul barks in his gruff voice.

HORRORific Tales   (Cryptids)

The seven of us form an arc facing him. I pull Katalina into my trembling arms and kiss the top of her head. The other maidens watch us, frowns on their stricken faces. I hope the monster chooses one of them. Anyone but my sister.

My stomach heaves as I release Katalina. Maybe I'm just as much a monster as Cherufe for wishing death on the other maidens. I should be sacrificed for even thinking such a thing.

Silence slithers into my ears. Even Katalina's sobs have faded to soundless cries. Being this close to Monte Cherufe, my nose twitches from volcanic gas and earthy notes perfuming the sweltering air. My gown clings to my damp flesh, from my neck to my ankles. Each breath of the toxic air slides down my throat and settles in my lungs.

Chief Raul inclines his chin, and his dark eyes flicker over each of us in turn. When they pause on me, my skin crawls. He doesn't utter another word. All of us know how this goes. There's no point dragging out the dread.

Once Chief Raul finishes inspecting us like we're less than human, he crouches next to the trench and dips the obsidian basin into the magma. Orange liquid fills the bowl to the brim. The magma glows brighter and brighter, blending with the sunset's colors, then transforms into crystalline water.

My spine stiffens. This is it. I only need to drink from the basin one last time.

Chief Raul approaches the first maiden on the far left. She holds out quivering hands, and he passes her the basin. Tears roll down her cheeks and rain into the enchanted water. Whimpering, she brings the bowl to her lips and sips. Clear water drizzles down her chin, and she weeps with relief.

My stomach lurches. Cherufe didn't choose her.

I gather my gown's cotton in my fists. Two more maidens are before me. Maybe one of them will be selected.

The next girl drinks from the basin.

Clear water.

HORRORific Tales   (Cryptids)

Despite the stifling heat, goosebumps bloom on my arms. I grab Katalina's hand and squeeze her clammy fingers. She'll be okay. We'll both be okay.

The maiden beside me presses her mouth against the basin's edge. She keeps her lips sealed, her body rigid.

My knees wobble. Drink already. Please.

Squeezing her eyes shut, she parts her lips and sips.

Clear water.

No. No. No.

Katalina grips my hand so hard, my bones threaten to break. Only four of us are left.

Diosavola, please let both my sister and me survive.

Chief Raul holds the basin toward me. I give Katalina's hand a final squeeze, then take the bowl for the last time. Katalina covers her mouth, her ocean eyes wide. I wish I could promise we'll both be okay, but those would be empty words.

I raise the basin to my face. My reflection ripples on the water's surface, blurry and distorted. Before me, Monte Cherufe stands like a looming silhouette against the sunset. Deep within the volcano, the monster is waiting.

For me?

I curl my toes into the ground. Sharp rocks pierce my skin, and I welcome the pain. It's a brief distraction from the tightness building in my chest.

But I can't stall anymore. Prolonging the unknown won't change my fate. Either Cherufe chose me, or he didn't.

"Please, Diosavola," I whisper.

Bracing myself, I touch my lips to the basin's brim and tilt the bowl. Icy liquid pours into my mouth, over my dry tongue, and down my throat.

Clear water.

Not magma.

I'm free. Tears cascade down my cheeks. I'm free. Free. Free.

HORRORific Tales   (Cryptids)

Tonight, I'll finally be with Silvio the way I've dreamed. Cherufe no longer has any claim to me.

But I can't celebrate. Not yet.

I pass the basin back to Chief Raul, then throw my arms around Katalina. Her small form shakes in my embrace. My little sister needs to survive her first Solsticio de Sacrificio. If she doesn't—

No, I can't imagine a future without her. She won't die.

"I love you, Kat," I whisper into her ear. "I'm right here."

I clutch her against me for a final beat, then let go. After wiping away tears, she takes the basin from Chief Raul and closes her eyes.

My thumping heart fills my ears. Katalina's fate is in Diosavola's divine hands now.

Clear water. Clear water. Clear water. Please. Clear water.

Katalina raises the bowl to her mouth. I want to look away, but I can't.

Please. Clear water.

My sister sips.

The water transforms into magma and burns her lips.

"No!" My cry blends with Katalina's screams.

I clutch my stomach. Not Katalina. This must be a mistake. Cherufe didn't choose her.

The basin slips from my sister's grasp and thumps to the ground. Magma pools at her feet. Skin peels from her burnt lips, as though the monster has sealed her fate with a searing kiss.

Cherufe has marked Katalina as his chosen sacrifice.

My wail rings through the valley as I sink to the ground. Why Katalina? Is the goddess punishing me for wishing death on the other maidens? Maybe this is all my fault. My fault. My fault.

Katalina collapses into a heap, hands folded over her ruined mouth. The five others stampede up the valley's slope, their footsteps growing fainter, until they fade into the wind. Katalina and I should be among them. My sister shouldn't be at the end of her short life. I want to hug her close, but I'm frozen.

HORRORific Tales   (Cryptids)

Chief Raul reaches into the depth of his robes and retrieves a white cloth. My body jolts. I won't watch Katalina get wrapped up in the material and carried to the volcano.

"I'll be the sacrifice." I shove myself to my feet and step toward Chief Raul.

"No, Mailyn," Katalina whimpers. My chest squeezes. How can she even speak with her burnt lips?

I straighten my spine. "I'm not letting him take you, Kat."

Chief Raul raises the white cloth. "Cherufe made his choice."

I round on him. "You're not going to carry my sister to her death. Cherufe wants a maiden sacrifice. I'll go in Katalina's place."

He shakes his head. "No. As I said, Cherufe made his choice. Katalina should feel proud."

"Proud?" My jaw drops.

"Yes, proud." He scrunches his wrinkled face. "Being sacrificed to spare our home from eruptions and earthquakes is a great honor."

I clench my fists so hard; my nails carve crescent moons into my skin. "If you think it's such an honor, why don't you throw yourself into the volcano?"

He levels me with a cold stare. "You know as well as I do that the magma is binding. It must be Katalina."

The weight of the truth digs its sharp claws into my shoulders. I open my mouth to argue further, but no words come out. The magma has been cursed by Cherufe to mark his chosen maidens for centuries. Why should the ceremony's ancient rules change just because my sister is the unlucky one? Tears sting my eyes. Before I can move a muscle, Chief Raul wraps Katalina in the white cloth and lifts her into his arms.

"Kat!" I lunge for her. My foot catches on a large rock, and I crash to the ground. I hardly register the pain shooting through my palms and knees.

The cloth muffles Katalina's screams and cries. I want to pray for Diosavola to grant a miracle, but I don't. I've lost all faith in the goddess. Katalina hasn't done a single thing to deserve this. She has the purest soul. Maybe that's why Cherufe desires her.

Chief Raul adjusts his grip on Katalina, then leaps over the magma trench.

"No." I slump to the ground. "No. Kat."

Tremors course through my veins as my sister is carried away from me, until she and Chief Raul are only a dot of color approaching the blackened volcano.

She's going to die. My sweet angel is going to die.

I scream into my hands until my voice is hoarse.

"Mailyn!"

The voice reaches me from far away. I face the rocky slope, but tears blur my vision.

"Mailyn!"

Silvio?

I blink. The haze veiling my eyes dissipates. Silvio races toward me, his emerald robes blowing around his muscular form.

I want to be elated to see him, but I'm numb. Cherufe will soon devour my sister. I'll never feel happiness again.

"Mailyn, thank Diosavola." Silvio drops beside me and cradles my limp body against him. His pinewood scent wafts up my nose, and for a moment, I fool myself into believing I'm not sitting beside the magma trench.

But I am.

And my sister is never coming back.

"Katalina," I cry into Silvio's shoulder.

"I'm so sorry." His voice cracks, and he holds me tighter. "When the five others returned, I knew one of you..."

"I wanted to go in her place." Sobs burst from my throat. "But I couldn't. Cherufe chose her."

Silvio runs his fingers along my braid. "I know. What can I do? Tell me what I can do."

Nothing. He can't do a single thing.

But I can.

I pull out of his embrace and glare at the volcano. Rage flows through my veins like the magma in the trench only feet away. Time isn't up yet, not until Chief Raul tosses my sister into Cherufe's lair. I refuse to weep in Silvio's arms when Katalina needs me. Curse the ancient tradition. I'm done playing by the monster's vicious rules.

I march toward the trench.

"Where are you going?" Silvio hurries after me. The glow from the magma coats his olive skin golden.

"I'm saving Katalina."

"What? No, you can't." He grabs my hand before I can cross the barrier. "Interfering with the sacrifice will have consequences. Cherufe might come for you."

"Let him try."

"Mailyn, I love you. Please don't do this. Stay. I promise I'll be here for you however you need me to be."

The desperation in his eyes almost makes me change my mind.

Almost.

Swallowing hard, I lean onto my tiptoes and press my lips against his. I could have a lifetime of kisses with him, but his love wouldn't be enough to fill the hole Katalina's death would leave behind. I need to stop her sacrifice.

Wishing this moment could last forever, I force myself to break the kiss. "I love you."

Before Silvio can stop me, I jump over the magma trench.

"Mailyn!"

I stumble, my heart cleaved in two. Silvio screams my name again and again, but I don't look back at him.

I run.

Broken rocks slice my feet as I race toward Monte Cherufe. Heat blasts my face, like I'm sprinting straight into hell. The volcanic gas thickens, and I choke. In a deep corner of my mind, I know what I'm doing is beyond the realm of insanity, but the monster left me no choice.

Out of breath, I reach the base of the volcano. I search above for Chief Raul and Katalina, but the mist is too thick. Even though they have a head start, I'll be able to move faster than the Lavasores' leader carrying my sister. I have a chance.

Gritting my teeth, I dig my nails into the crumbling black rock forming the volcano and climb. My muscles strain, but I inch higher, and higher, and higher. The closer I ascend toward the yawning opening into Cherufe's home, the steeper the volcano becomes.

HORRORific Tales   (Cryptids)

My hand slips. Gasping, I fight to regain my grip on the rocks. If I fall, I'll shatter bones, maybe even die on impact.

How much farther?

I squint through the gray fumes. The sunset's bold colors are hardly visible through the veil. I don't have a hope of spotting the summit, but I keep climbing. Sooner or later, I'll reach the top.

A shriek pierces the silence.

"Katalina!"

Chief Raul must have thrown her into the volcano.

I'm too late.

She's gone.

I scream like I never have before. If I would have gone after my sister right away instead of falling apart, instead of kissing Silvio, maybe I could have saved her in time.

The volcano rumbles.

My hands slide off the rocks. Panting, I try to anchor myself with my feet.

Monte Cherufe shakes harder.

My aching toes slip from their crevices, and I tumble down the volcano.

I wince each time my body collides with the sharp rocks. Dark spots speckle my vision. My skin stings from deep gashes on my arms. Hot blood trickles down my face from a cut in the center of my forehead.

I slam into solid ground. The sunset fades in and out of focus. Every inch of my body aches. Dirt smears my torn gown. Open wounds, blood, and blooming bruises cover my skin.

My heart hurts the most. Half of it died when Katalina met her end in the volcano.

The ground trembles. Is Cherufe causing an earthquake? No. He got his sacrifice. My sister.

Unless Silvio is right, and the monster is angry I attempted to change Katalina's fate.

A blurry figure flies past me. Aqua robes. Gray beard.

Chief Raul.

He doesn't even spare me a glance, just bolts toward the trench.

I clench my jaw and suppress a moan. At least one bone in my face is broken. If I had the strength to move, I would have darted after Chief Raul and shoved him into the magma.

"Mailyn!"

Silvio's cry floats to me in the wind.

"Mailyn! Run!"

Run? I shift on the ground and stabbing pain jolts through my bones.

Gold wavers in the corner of my eye. Whimpering, I tilt my head.

A river of lava flows down the volcano, coming straight for me.

My heart hammers against my broken ribs. I need to move. Now.

Steeling myself for the agony, I scramble to my feet and take off toward the barrier. I channel all my focus into staying upright. How I'm managing that, I'm unsure. I must be running on pure adrenaline. The lava won't reach me. It won't.

Silvio comes into view. When his eyes lock with mine, a tortured wail soars from between his lips. Each movement sends flames through my veins, but I keep staggering toward safety.

"Mailyn, the lava! Hurry!" Silvio holds his arms out.

Sweat soaks my back. I stumble the final distance to the trench, then bend over and clutch my ribs. Bracing myself, I peek over my shoulder.

A scream seizes my throat.

The lava is only feet from me.

"Jump!" Silvio extends his hands farther. "Jump, Mailyn!"

Heat blazes around my ankles.

I'm out of time.

HORRORific Tales   (Cryptids)

Squeezing my eyes shut, I launch myself into the air. Screams tear from my throat and reverberate off the rocks. My stomach swoops. What if I didn't jump far enough, and I drop into the magma?

Strong hands grab my waist.

Silvio. He has me. I'm safe. My screams dissolve into wheezing coughs.

Something hot and sticky wraps around my ankles. It can't be the lava. I screech and kick my feet.

"No!" Silvio yanks me closer, but the sticky thing tugs me back.

My feet feel as though I've dipped them in the magma trench. I twist in Silvio's grip to see what has a hold of me. Bile creeps up my throat, and I choke it back down.

A gold tongue coils around my ankles and traces all the way up the volcano, disappearing into the haze.

Cherufe's tongue.

Silvio and the monster pull me in opposite directions like I'm nothing more than a rag doll. If they continue this, I'll get torn in two.

I wrap my arms around Silvio and hold on for dear life. My hand bumps something hard in his pocket.

His hunting knife.

I gulp. This is my only hope.

I shove my hand into Silvio's pocket and pull out the carved blade.

"Turn me around," I tell Silvio as Cherufe gives another powerful tug with his disgusting tongue.

"What? But—"

"Trust me."

Squeezing my waist, Silvio flips me over. The gold tongue tightens its grip. My toes tingle from the blocked circulation.

With my spine pressed against Silvio's front, I draw my knees to my chest. Sweat and blood drip into my eyes. The knife grows slick in my grasp, but I don't drop it. Gray tinges my vision. If I pass out, it's over for me.

This is for choosing Katalina, I hiss to the monster in my head, and somehow, I know he hears me.

HORRORific Tales						(Cryptids)

I swing my arm forward. The knife slices through Cherufe's tongue. Silvio stumbles backwards, and we collapse to the ground, our limbs tangled.

The monster's roar shakes the valley. Lava pours from the volcano. The tongue retreats, speckling the black rocks with golden blood. Too bad the monster didn't fully emerge from his lair. If he had, I would have chopped off his reptilian head and put an end to the maiden sacrifices.

Fighting back vomit, I peel the tongue's tip off me and toss it into the trench, where it hits the magma with a splash. Rings of burnt, raw flesh circle my ankles.

The valley shudders once more, then falls still.

My adrenaline rush fades, and I become limp in Silvio's arms. I may have sliced Cherufe's tongue to free myself, but Silvio saved me. If he hadn't been waiting beside the magma trench, Cherufe's tongue would have carried me into the monster's mouth.

A large rock hits the magma with a clunk. The flaming liquid sprays Silvio and me, and we flinch. Gasping, he scoops me up and staggers to his feet. The rock bobs on the magma's surface as it flows by us.

Not a rock.

Burnt flesh clings to a blackened skull.

A head.

Katalina's head.

I twist in Silvio's arms and throw up over and over again, until I'm only dry heaving. Cherufe devoured my sister's body and left her head, the way he always does with his maiden sacrifices.

A sound I didn't think I was capable of making rips from my raw throat. Silvio murmurs words I can't make out. I rest my bloody cheek against his chest and focus on the familiar rhythm of his heartbeat.

Never in my wildest nightmares did I believe my last Solsticio de Sacrificio would unfold like this.

Katalina is dead.

I almost met the same fate.

In time, my injuries will fade and scar, but the loss of Katalina will never fully heal.

Silvio rubs circles on my back as he carries me up the slope, and I don't have the heart to tell him his gentle motions hurt. His words from before I leapt over the magma trench replay in my ears.

HORRORific Tales   (Cryptids)

I promise I'll be here for you however you need me to be.

I believe him. Somehow, I got blessed with the most wonderful man, and I can finally embrace a future with him.

But from now on, when I look at Monte Cherufe, I'll relive the worst night of my life. I didn't venture through death's door, but this isn't freedom, not with Katalina gone. Someday, somehow, I'll find a way to kill the monster for taking my sister away from me, even if it's the last thing I do.

Check out Demi's work here:

The Shadow of Slieveanorra

by
Colin C Martin

HORRORific Tales   (Cryptids)

Shredded canvas and various other materials littered the campsite. It was something resembling a lawnmower ploughing through the middle of the place Inspector Steven Mullan thought grimly. He was approaching thirty years on the force. Having been a member of the RUC and now PSNI he had seen his fair share of tragedy over the years, including some of the worst atrocities that people could inflict on each other. The scene that lay before him was as bewildering as it was horrifying.

This area of Glenariff Forest Park was a popular camping spot with locals and tourists. It was marked on the Ulster Way, a well-known walking trail, used regularly throughout the year. Many tens of thousands of people had spent time in this area over the years. This kind of attack was simply unheard of. The Inspector found himself holding back vomit as he surveyed the scene.

In amongst the ripped fabric were the entrails of what he assumed to be the family that was spending the night there. Judging by the size of the tent, there were at least four to six people that were staying in it. V-Checks carried out on the handful of vehicles in the carpark were quickly traced to their owners barring the Peugeot 5008 which belonged to a rental company.

They would have to wait until the local office opened at 09:00 to get access to their customer database and identify the occupants. The SOCO's and Forensic teams had marked off the area just as the sun had finished rising. At this point they had covered at least 2 hectares of forest before they stopped finding body parts.

This wasn't an animal attack, Mullan was sure of that. He had found plenty of bodies over the years. Some of the worst he had found was when, say for example the body of an informant had been left in an abandoned house in one of either the hardline Loyalist or Republican estates. It was usually rats that got to the body before either local kids discovered it or the police received a tip off. The paramilitaries wanted the bodies to be found. It was an effect message to send to those in their areas who were considering becoming 'touts'. The worse state that the body was found helped to strengthen that message. There was an understanding among family and mourners when a closed coffin funeral had to take place.

HORRORific Tales   (Cryptids)

Mullan had done his stint in both the Bogside and Waterside of Londonderry when he was toying with the idea of applying for Special Branch. Two years of watching the various factions try to outdo each other with their levels of brutality helped him decide that the quiet life, well as quiet as the life of a police officer could be here wasn't so bad. He had done quite well for himself considering. The Antrim area still had plenty of crime to solve. He was respected by his colleagues and his calm, investigative approach brought results. He rose through the ranks of CID to the position he was in now. Covering a tourist area before retirement was meant to be his chance to wind down. There was going to be no winding down today.

"Guv! We need you here." One of the Forensic officers called to him. Gallagher was a good scene of crimes man and Mullan had worked with him a lot over the years. He wasn't prone to overexcitement or outbursts and never called for the officer in charge until he had something worthy to report. Something was up for him to call at this stage. He made his way over to the entrance of the forest being careful not to scratch himself on the pine needles.

Mullan gingerly stepped around the flags that had been placed in the ground which marked pools of blood and tiny flecks of human material. One of the globules of what he assumed was fat caught his eye, the morning sun poking through the trees reflecting of the round membrane. 'What on earth did this?' He thought grimly.

"Please tell me, that it's not any worse!" Mullan almost pleaded with the forensics officer. Bill Gallagher was a steadfast individual who didn't embellish his reports. It was something that the Inspector found to be a reliable and comforting trait. "I really wish that I could say that Steve", he answered. The apparent over familiarity whilst on an active investigation by dropping ranks was not lost on Mullan. He was being softened up. "You need to see this", the officer said flatly. "Frankly I don't know how to describe it."

The Inspector was led into a small clearing in a patch of wood. What would normally have been moss covered rocked looked as if they had been cleaned, polished and arranged in a circle. There was something unnatural, yet natural about the setting. It had obviously been man made, yet somehow the rocks looked like they had been there since before even this 50,000-year-old forest sprang to life. The cairn at the centre of the stone ring had definitely been made by someone. As his eyes glanced over to it Mullan couldn't help but let out a gasp.

Despite having witnessed practically every form of cruelty that could be inflicted on another person he had never actually seen a human face scalped from its body before.

Arranged meticulously between the rocks of the cairn were the faces of people. Some were worn and leather like as if they had been there for decades. Others were fresher, but still obviously years old. *Surely this can't be real*, Mullan thought. The setup looked like something the special effects team from a horror movie would put together. Were local film students pulling a prank? It wasn't until he walked to where his forensics officer was standing that the reality of the situation hit him.

Nestled in amongst the older leather and dried husks were new offerings. The pasty white sheen of the family skin stood out in stark contrast to the more 'settled in' residents. It was a family, Mullan was sure of that. Even with basic bone structure being replaced by the jagged rocks beneath the skin he could still see the resemblance. Mother, father, son, daughter and…

Baby.

It wasn't a newborn but couldn't have been more than a year old. Mullan choked as the meaning of the scene began to register in his brain. This wasn't an animal attack, random killing or even a paramilitary execution. This was a ritual, something ancient that had been going on before anyone here had even been born. The reverence with which the faces had been placed on the cairn was a testament to that. Apart from one or two drops of fresh blood the stones were spotless. Even after placement, this structure was maintained. No moss grew on the stones or offerings. He understood the display for what it was now. This would mean daily cleaning of the area. Were the skinned faces taken off, treated and replaced again? That would require careful work and dedication, far beyond that of just a single killer. Even well-known killers of the time, Shipman, West, Moat hadn't been that methodical. No, this was religious practice displayed before him. Devout and fanatical.

HORRORific Tales   (Cryptids)

"I swear to God, even if I have to put the army back on the streets, we are going to find the bastards that did this", Mullan practically growled. It was an empty threat of course. The ceasefire had been in place for over twenty years at this point. It would take an Act of Parliament to decide like that. Any Prime Minister that made that call was aware of the fact that their career would be over. Despite the atrocities that were swept under the rug every year 'peace' remained in Northern Ireland. For the first time in his life the Inspector wanted to lash out, go out and kick doors down and squeeze the information out of people until he found the culprits. Was this a cult? How have they been able to operate for so long without being discovered? Where were they operating from? Cushendun, Crommelin? It couldn't be Armoy, their religion was the Northwest 200!

Mullan surprised himself at how quickly and easily the gallows' humour rose to the surface. It was a defense mechanism employed by many of those in the services to deal with the daily trauma of encountering the worst humanity had to offer. He strategically snorted to cover up his chuckle, lest he didn't appear to be disrespectful of the tragedy that lay before him. "What do you think this is Bill", Mullan asked, returning the familiarity that his colleague had displayed. "A pagan group?

Satanists?" He was at a loss to put a name to those who could carry this out. "I really am at a loss Sir", Gallagher answered, a measure of defeat in his voice. "I'm no historian, but the only evidence of ritual sacrifices ever found here have been the ancient bog bodies. Everyone knows that. Nothing like this!" Even Gallagher was finding it difficult to keep a tremble out of his voice.

Mullan nodded. He was right of course. Even in the twenty first century mummified remains of bound bodies were still being found. Cutting turf for peat logs was still a tradition here, carried out by tractor these days rather than by hand. The fuel was still utilised by rural communities and by people who had open fires in their homes. Places like the Giant's Ring close to Belfast were suspected to have been used for ritual sacrifice, but nothing obvious like the grand altars or tables found in other parts of the world. There was a practically and simplicity in which the way death was dealt to others in this land. Every Ulsterman and woman knew that to their core. That carried more menace and dread than the loud banging of drums or flowing of robes could ever hope to.

HORRORific Tales (Cryptids)

With the initial shock receding, the analytical mind of the detective taking over, Mullan surveyed the area. One thing that hadn't registered with him coming into the place was the lack of midges in the clearing. You almost got used to the biting little bastards when operating in the countryside. They came as part of the package. Carnages such as this brought them out in droves. He sniffed and was rewarded with the overpowering smell of Lavender. Looking around the clearing floor he noticed the abundant sprigs planted there. In older times before the advent of mosquito spray and Citronella candles, handfuls of this herb were bunched into 'posies' and hung above babies' cots. The old wife's tale was that they warded off demons. In practical terms it helped to keep biting insects away from their infants.

"This area has been cleared and planted as an offering", Mullan mused out loud. Looking clearly now, he could see the laid-out garden that was plotted. Now that he was paying attention, he could see the stark contrast between this area and the wild countryside surrounding it. Was the chaotic throwing of the body parts outside of this area part of the ritual then? Normally offerings were made to a deity. This could be personified by a location or even in something like the sun. A Pagan offering was usually to nature, the change of the seasons representing a God or Goddess. Mullan looked around again and glanced between the trees.

Despite being less than a kilometre tall the summit of Slieveanorra loomed above them. The surrounding forests and hills almost seemed to bow towards the lonely hill. Until this moment the Inspector hadn't thought about it in that way before. Now it seemed obvious. Everything in the area existed in subservience to the small mountain. Mullan could feel it now. It was almost as if a watchful eye was cast over them now, observing with disapproval. A gentle cough from his colleague brought him back to reality.

"Sir, with your permission we will start gathering in the remains for evidence and analyses", Gallagher said. "We can carry out DNA testing on these…" He pointed briefly towards the macabre display of human faces. "To determine if any or all are human. We can carbon date these to determine the age and potentially the frequency of these acts." Mullan noted how the Forensics Officer cleverly avoided saying, "Ritual human sacrifices that have been taking place in the same place for thousands of years, right under our noses!"

HORRORific Tales   (Cryptids)

"Carry on", Mullan said simply. He had the sudden urge to get out of here now, back to a village or housing estate. Anywhere with technology, a TV, a radio, a kettle even. Anything to remind him that he still lived in modern society and not some medieval hellscape where Druids marched families up to hills and slaughtered them as offerings to the sun or moon and God knows what else just so that they'd have nice weather or whatever they asked for. 'I haven't been to church in a while. I think this Sunday would be a good time to visit', He mused.

It took the best part of the day to work from the perimeter inwards collecting the remains. Every spot was marked, numbered and photographed before each piece of the victim could be collected in evidence bags to be brought back to the lab. This of course would only be the part of the process. Weeks of testing lay ahead to match the remains to each victim, as well as determining whether any parts had been removed or added. This might also help in figuring out which sect, cult or religious practice was being carried out here. There was no doubt that this was going to make the news and be the subject of many a discussion for years to come. Mullan wasn't worried about any of that now. The day was fading fast.

It was twilight when the teams finally made it to the ritual area. Despite being normal protocol to search outwards, establish a perimeter, then work back towards the main crime scene, it also felt right to leave this abomination to last before tackling it. Inspector Mullan couldn't help but stare at the thing in morbid fascination. Even after it was taken down the image of what stood before him would be burned into his memory forever.

"I guess it's time to start taking this apart then", Gallagher almost whispered. "The sensible course of action would be to start from the top of the cairn and work downwards in case there is a collapse. If there is we will have at least gathered the most recent remains who still have families that need to be informed."

"I want to kick the bloody thing over now!" Mullan growled. Detectives had come back with IDs on the potential victims during the day. The car had been rented out by the Goossens family from Belgium. They were on a touring holiday of the British Isles. Alexandre and Jacquelynne had been married for ten years with their two boys Amdt and Nicholas. Their baby girl Gaella was seven months old.

HORRORific Tales   (Cryptids)

"I know how you feel about this one boss!" Gallagher said. "We've seen a lot over the years, but this is a bit much even for me. Let's get this done and grab a pint. I don't know about you, but I need one." Mullan smiled grimly and nodded in reply.

The Forensic Officers worked in pairs. One lifted a face from the cairn while the other held open a marked evidence bag for it to be deposited in. Free standing decorators' ladders had to be brought in as the ground was too uneven for the usual platforms. They couldn't risk leaning anything against the cairn in case the whole structure collapsed, destroying valuable evidence and potentially causing injury.

The howling didn't register with the team until they had cleared half of the cairn from its gruesome ornamentation. Living in a rural area, the calls of the various wildlife and farm animals was a normal way of things. This included sheepdogs, foxes and other animals that resided in the area. This was usually their time to call out and mark their territories.

The first screams brought everyone to alert. These weren't cries of pain or fear, but almost like shouts of rage. Not quite human, but almost. Mullan unsnapped his Ruger Speed-Six from its holster and motioned for the Forensic team to start making their way to the cordon where other officers would be waiting. With his free hand he radioed the duty sergeant at the scene. "Bring the TSGs forward", he said. "I think we have company."

With an operation as large at this at least three land rovers would be standing by in case of civil disorder or a dissident attack. Each carried an armed team of six officers ready to respond. It was at times like this that the Inspector missed having the army on hand. They would have been placed out in the surrounding fields as they were trained to work in the environment. *A helicopter or two would be handy right now,* he thought.

The rustling throughout the forest grew louder and more intense as it became obvious that multiple figures were running towards the ritual site. 'Even the locals wouldn't be stupid enough to try and rush into a full police operation, would they?' "Hello, all callsigns this is Delta India One. Stand to, I repeat stand to. Unknown ICs entering cordon. Charlie Whiskey Zero One to my location. Over."

HORRORific Tales (Cryptids)

"Roger Out." The curt, crisp response from the first Tactical Support Group Land Rover meant that a heavily armed team would be moving at speed towards him. The vehicles could make it most of the way up the track before the officers would have to dismount and rush to him on foot. The other two vehicles would automatically make their way to the outer cordon whilst letting control know that the situation had escalated. In a short amount of time this area would be swarming with assets. Steven Mullan stood proudly knowing that he held the rank of Inspector in one of the most elite police forces in the world. A borderline force, forged in conflict and simultaneously trained to deal with the extremes of terrorism whilst also providing the necessities of community support which helped to maintain law and order and a cohesive society. Forces from around the globe regularly sent liaisons to learn about this unique skill set and try to apply it in their own countries. They were the envy of every other constabulary and ready to deal with anything.

A nagging thought told Mullan that they might not be ready to deal with this.

The first crack of a pistol round and a scream confirmed his fears. As the light faded Mullan tried to figure out which of his officers had been attacked. Constables MacLaughlin and Carson were on the left flank. It could be one of them. Another scream on the left this time. Davidson or Graham. 'How many people are part of this crazy bastard cult?' Mullan growled to himself.

The sound of boots and flashes of Maglites strengthened his resolve. They could move forward and deal with the casualties.

"ARMED POLICE, DON'T MOVE! AGHHHHH!"

Multiple screams from behind him sent ice cold sweat dripping down the Inspector's spine. The TSG didn't even manage to fire a round before being cut down. This couldn't be happening, no one moves that fast. For the first time in decades, panic and fear started to overwhelm him.

HORRORific Tales (Cryptids)

Mullan wasn't sure if it was the lighting or the adrenaline coursing through his veins, but he could almost swear that the eyes of the things that emerged were glowing amber. They weren't animals, well not exactly. They stood roughly five feet in height on two legs. They weren't quite apes either, although outside of a zoo or nature documentary Mullan wasn't exactly sure what to expect if he was encountering a pack of them in the wild.

They weren't clothed. Hair covered their entire body. Mullan couldn't quite place what animals they could be related to. They weren't bears, although their hands did extend out into claws. Their faces were closer to human than ape. The hair that covered their face and head was long and flowing. Not even remotely close to the fur of an animal he could recognise. The sight before him was as confusing as it was frightening.

They formed a circle at the edge of the clearing, watching him intently. It was at this moment that Mullan realised why he was still alive. He was standing in their ritual circle; they didn't want to cross over and desecrate their place of worship. Then which one….

Pain erupted in Mullan's back and he shrieked in agony. He felt the hot breath of the creature that jabbed its claws into his spine. Blood filled his mouth, and he began to choke as the clawed hand tore into his stomach, wrenching his vital organs from him. He fell forward coughing and crying as he felt his life swiftly begin to slip away. He felt the hot breath on his neck again as the thing that had sneaked up on him pressed its lips to his ear. "fear-salachair an ionaid naoimh" were the last words he heard before slipping into oblivion.

Check out Colin's work here:

HORRORific Tales   (Cryptids)

Eyja Beinannar -
The Island Of the Bones

by
Eli Beals

HORRORific Tales   (Cryptids)

The storm descended like an ungodly hammer on us. My boat was not made for this kind of chop and it was only a matter of time until the hammer would blast it into slag.

Sure enough on the descent from a forty foot swell I over corrected and the rudder was practically ripped from the hull from extreme turbulence and the next wave was already rising to greet us.

Jackson looked at me then, his eyes as wide as saucers knowing what it meant. We were going into the soup, nothing to be done about it.

All we could do in those moments was hold on to something and pray.

Something intervened in the way a passing train can stop a breakaway horse, by sheer mass.

Not sure how fast we could have been going when the collision happened, but it must've been fast because the impact launched Jackson clear through the glass, out of the bridge and into darkness. He didn't even scream.

Maybe I did, though, until at least something hard and heavy broke loose and knocked me out cold.

I awoke half submerged in water amidst the wreckage of the SS Lenore and upon seeing Jackson there on land I thought what a strange position to be napping in. That is, until I recalled the event that brought us here. The look on his face as he rocketed out of the boat, seeing his scalp peel away from the razor edges of shattered glass as if time had slowed just enough to burn those images into my memory.

I've been sailing these waters for a good long while now, and this island was not in any of my internal maps, which made me wonder how far we could have been blown off course.

Before I could tend to my friend, I had to see what supplies washed ashore with me and what sort of trouble I was really in.

A short walk down shore revealed the red and white bundle that filled me with relief, knowing there was at least a few days' worth of life packed away.

The irony never seems to lose its barb when it comes to water out at sea. Surrounded by countless gallons, and none of it drinkable. It might as well be a desert, maybe even worse.

HORRORific Tales (Cryptids)

There is no greater sensation in the world than drinking fresh cold water on the verge of dehydration. The trick is to drink slowly, allowing it to seep into your husking cells. Sometimes a person will vomit it right out if they take it in too fast. So I went slow, savoring each renewing sip.

The headache diminished almost immediately, save for the sore lump on my forehead where I was concussed.

Thinking a little clearer I began to take note in greater detail of my surroundings. Particularly the tidepool that I had retrieved the emergency pack from.

Everything that skittered, swam or clung to the rock was a sickly pale hue, as if any color it might have had, was bleached out of it. The kind of thing you'd see on the deep ocean floor. Like everything else on this island I thought, as if it was all made of bone left in the sun for a decade then drowned in the depths. It was alien to me.

Fashioned from a gaffing hook and fiberglass hull, the shovel bit into the mealy pale soil with little effort to complete the grim task of burying my longtime business partner and friend. Why I decided that it was something I had to do did not occur to me then, an optimist would have just covered them, and maybe there was a part of me that knew that help would not be coming any time soon.

I could only dig a few feet down before I hit rock, which explained the lack of trees or any plant life save for the carpet of stiff brush flowered with pale indigo petals, the only real color in this place. The shallow grave was more of a mound, but it was the best I could do for him, as for his preferences he once told me that he liked the idea of having his ashes scattered in the mediterranean.

Jackson's eulogy was mostly me apologizing for my part in his death. Knowing that it was a risk we took each time we went out to catch our haul. Had we known that such a squall would bear down on us, would we still go? No, and to that fact I was innocent, yet I still felt the guilt the survivor often does.

HORRORific Tales (Cryptids)

The rest of the day I spent resting and scraping dry wood into kindling so that I could make a fire in hopes that any passing boats or low flying planes might see me out here.

I had never been stranded like this before but have read my fair share of stories about it which lead me to some self-delusion that all of this was kind of romantic. The solitude and primitive mechanics of basic survival brought to the forefront as some kind of biological imperative.

I had to admit that I was kind of enjoying it. I fell asleep with a belly full of peanut butter protein bar near a cheerful fire and dreamed of cheeseburgers.

When I woke, my disappointment evaporated with a sense there was something wrong.

It took a minute or so to realize that the sun was in the wrong place. Either it rose in the south now, or that the island itself had somehow rotated. Both of these were so contradictory to my understanding of reality that I rationalized it to delirium brought about by dehydration. Yet in the back of my mind a siren would not relent in its urgency. A steady message echoing through my skull, saying to get away from here.

Scanning the horizon yielded no feature or hope that aid was forthcoming, so I hiked across to see if there was anything on this island that I could burn to make my fire bigger, more visible.

Down to two litres of water, I had to be careful and could probably fashion some kind of evaporator to purify the sea water, but I was not that desperate yet.

The island was about a half mile or so across and maybe a mile long bearing a single hill on the East Side, yet my brain screamed that only yesterday it was on the North side.

The hill reached an elevation of about twenty-five feet and I realized that it was not a hill at all, it was a ship.

Overgrown with the scrub that blanketed the interior of this place I could see upon closer inspection that it was very old. My first thought was if I could get it to burn it would make for a great signal fire, but it was practically crumbling and rotting so it would not burn for very long if at all. If I had to guess it was a small frigate, two masts half buried and pointing like accusing fingers toward the ocean that wrecked her. Or maybe it was this island that imposed itself?

HORRORific Tales (Cryptids)

While gathering I attempted to pry a rectangular piece that seemed dry enough when it creaked open on rusty hinges revealing the contents of a chest.

Nothing of much use really, just relics of a bygone age. An empty oil lamp, articles of brittle clothing and sundries, and an oil skin wrapped journal written in some kind of Norse language that I later would learn was Icelandic.

Flipping through the pages I could see sketches of various things. A frequent image of a woman, maybe a wife they were trying not to forget the face of? The illustrations began turning into stranger compositions. Sea monsters and the like. The writing progressed from a neat and skilled script to near illegible scrawls. The final entry was dated Juni 1790, I assumed it was June, and several times a phrase repeated. Eyja Beinanna, though I could not translate it I could however glean from the way it was penned that this person wrote these words with mounting apprehension. The trembling characters transferred the author's anxiety to me through the centuries that were then frothing in my guts.

Piling the wood on a tattered wool blanket I dragged the load back to my camp to rebuild the signal fire.

Days passed in this fashion, gathering more wood, catching the various sea life trapped in the tidepools, wishing for some old bay seasoning.

Watching the sunset, letting its colors blur into a wash of tangerine and crimson through unfocused eyes viewing my past play out like a silent film. Cutting through the imaginary projection I saw something appear, a thick vertical silhouette bisecting the sun as it dipped beneath the curvature of the earth. Not knowing whether it was approaching or retreating, I scrambled to get more wood on the fire. After it was a roaring blaze. I sat and loaded a signal flare waiting with my gaze unblinking to where the sun had just gone down.

I must have sat there for hours in the desperate hope that any second, I would see the bright lights of rescue on its way, but none came. Perhaps it was my imagination, but I swear I heard a distant splash.

I had three flares yet resisted firing a single one that evening in fear of wasting one on a hallucination or a strange trick of the light.

Sleep did not come easy as despair whispered certain death in my ear while visions of monstrous creatures lurked just beyond the threshold of nightmares.

HORRORific Tales   (Cryptids)

Surviving can sometimes be a matter of doing nothing, conserving energy so that when it is needed it is there. And like the evaporated sea water condensing and dropping one tear at a time into my canteen I gathered myself to be ready.

How many days passed I cannot say, but much of that time I spent trying to make sense from the ancient journal left behind by a Crewman named Jon Einarsson. I looked for repetition of phrases or commonly used words to infer meaning. Which lent to some rough translation to which I can say that the ship was a whaling ship, and they were heading home without any success. That Jon Einarsson missed and loved his wife very much was evident by the many mentions in his entries but dwindled further on. Eventually the text strayed into more pressing matters, such as the shipwreck and much darker things. Things that desperate men do in such conditions just to keep living.

Even then as I slowly wasted away to skin and bone the thought of eating my friend did not occur to me. At the mere thought of him I glanced inland to where I had buried him and I noticed something was off, as if the mound had collapsed, creating a recess in the pale soil. Knowing that this was normal as something decomposes it loses mass in putrefaction. However, that voice in the back of my mind had become much louder and more insistent about these strange things in this strange place so I could not leave it be.

If only to appease my burning curiosity I went to exhume my friend and found no trace of him.

As if he were never there. Either that, or something had taken him.

That was the moment when I felt the threads of sanity start pulling apart. I wanted to jump into the water and swim as far away from here as I possibly could. After standing for a while gazing at that infinite expanse of ocean, an idea lit on me, one that I had not seriously considered. And a raft was certainly a better strategy than just flinging myself into the open sea. So, I got to work. I know that if I had waited even one more day, I would not be writing this now.

HORRORific Tales   (Cryptids)

It was as good a raft as could possibly be given the conditions and available materials. Most of it was made from the debris of SS Lenore, and it would keep me above the cold Atlantic barring any more wild storms. One way or another, the old boat would take me home.

With enough water to last a few days I pushed off from the shore taking only a few necessities with me, with one exception, Jon Einarssons journal which I had formed a deep connection to and if I ever made it home again, would have it translated properly as soon as possible.

The current was pulling west but I paddled against it just to gain some distance from that place as a growing unease was building, as if the thing I had just departed was aware of my absence and was watching me.

The shovel I made to bury Jackson served just well as an oar. Maybe from adrenaline or just the exhilaration of once again being afloat on the ocean I paddled hard. Exhaustion caught up to me eventually and when I turned to see how far I had gone, my heart sank. The island was still in sight, and not as far away as I would have hoped. Taking a few pulls of water and a handful of snail jerky that felt and tasted like salty rubber bullets I pressed on, the sense of malice emanating from the island was a constant companion at my back. At that point I was almost certain that the island was chasing me.

Each slice into the sea was another pull on the rack, another lash from the whip, another bamboo shoot under my nails, yet panic kept me going even when an unnatural fog coalesced around me, I kept my rhythm steady in painful hope to outrun it. The fog, so dense, I thought I could scoop a handful of it and drink from it.

The human body can only be pushed so far until it simply shuts down, especially without fuel, and I was running on fumes. Over the sound of my own ragged breathing, I could hear the deep drone of the ocean, that murmuring thrum of water in constant motion. Beneath that and faintly I could hear the waves breaking on those bone white shores.

Or was it engines? Did I see a pulse of electric light briefly flash through the shrouding mist? There it was again, a sweeping beam of light cutting a diffused tunnel through the miasma and energy flooded me once again.

HORRORific Tales					(Cryptids)

My pursuer must have also sensed the nearby vessel as a distinct vibration trembled through my haphazard craft. Transmitting some primal outburst that its prey was escaping. My oar tore deep into the water and once or twice I felt it scrape against something solid and grasping yet always just out of reach. Perhaps the sheer amount of water this leviathan was pushing was lending speed to me much to its own frustration as that tremble turned to an audible roar that sounded from deep beneath the surface.

My veins pumped acid from my machine gun heart and every breath was salty fire, yet I kept my pace steady and aimed relentlessly toward the light and the distant churn of diesel burning motors. I reached for the flare gun and fired a round up into the night, its throbbing pulses so brilliant that for a few moments I could see the bulk of my pursuer behind me through the fog and I gasped upon seeing a mere suggestion of its entirety. The island, merely a crown upon the countenance of a shapeless titan.

In the dying flares red light reflected two vast unblinking eyes that were staring directly at me and continued to stare as it slowly submerged until the light petered out.

It was letting me go.

Not trusting this odd sense of victory, I had over this primordial being I pressed on with what little strength left to me.

Then as I turned back to my heading. I was looking up at the deck full of astonished faces, none made any gesture and I wondered if it was in shock of seeing a half mad staved man adrift on a ramshackle raft or if they had seen what I did, then they began cheering.

I am not what you'd call a religious man, yet I waved and cried the tears of salvation as if I was witness to the second coming of the lord, and it might as well have been. Because I was saved.

They welcomed me with blankets and bottled water, and many, many questions but I think that was when I reached my threshold for consciousness and drifted on an entirely different sea for many hours.

I awoke a few times to see walls, order and the safety of modern convention, each time thanking a god I did not truly believe in, I was going home, that was enough.

HORRORific Tales   (Cryptids)

One of the crew must have discovered the journal I had tucked into my ragged shirt and had learned something that I could not decipher from its pages. He was all too friendly and skirted the issue with casual banter until he began to pry. And I was all too cooperative, being in their absolute debt, I spared no details, not thinking about his angle.

He asked me about the ship on the island and I told him what I saw then a gleam lit his eyes with excitement. Then I understood his intent to find the island, not to avoid it at any cost. My reaction was to warn him, but anything I said merely seemed to encourage that there was something there that I was trying to hide.

He set the journal on my cot where I lay and departed without another word, cooly regarding me with a gloating smile. Perhaps he thought I was trying to hide a wonder, a treasure beyond a common man's hopes with tales of sea monsters and certain peril.

They wouldn't listen to my warning, to them it may have seemed like ravings of a wretched castaway which I couldn't fault them for.

They left me at the port to the awaiting emergency response crew, and as the doors closed to the ambulance, I made my peace with it all, but maybe it was the effects of the sedative flooding my veins.

It was only a week until I saw the article, a commercial vessel with twenty-seven aboard had gone missing. All efforts to locate them had been called off and were presumed dead.

I tried to tell them, I really did. A few days after that the ship was found, adrift and crewless two hundred miles from the distant shores of Greenland, a ghost ship.

The realization that I wasn't a survivor, or a victim of circumstance dawned on me then. That some inscrutable god or the universe wasn't testing my mettle, my will to live or anything like that. It was that I served as the thrashing worm on a hook to attract bigger game. I was nothing more than bait.

Check out Eli's work here:

HORRORific Tales   (Cryptids)

Salivating, Drooling Evil

by
Arthur L

HORRORific Tales   (Cryptids)

Hatupatu had gone further into the forest than usual, his village more than a few hours' walk behind. They seldom went into this part of the forest because the pigs and birds were abundant nearer, there was no need to come this far. Besides, there were much easier parts to walk through. He had to force his way through leafy manuka branches and clamber round bulbous roots and thickets of flax to emerge in a bare path-like slip beside a small creek.

The more chaotic trees and sharper, tougher grasses had scratched him in many places over the last hour, with a little blood. Mostly scratches, but even blood for him to show off a bit.

He was proud he'd gone further than most of the hunters usually travelled, and his chest swelled outward. If he caught a pig, he'd have a great story to tell!

Someone must have been here before; perhaps the ladies of his village had taken some smaller trees from here many cycles ago. Strangely, the forest was a little thinner for no apparent reason. Its bareness allowed him some moments of reflection, and he breathed in the still, thick air, tasting the scents of foliage with his nose.

"Boy!" – A voice cried out, a man's voice, old, sharp, dry like a dead twig. A sudden snap.

Hatupatu's head spun; eyes searching, it took him a few seconds to see the origin. He was right next to a tall Rimu, one of the strongest woods in the world, and he reached out to touch it for balance. His feet slipped a little on the mud beneath as he shivered. He dug his pig-spear into the ground for balance, and not just for the balance of his body.

On the other side of the creek, the land tilted upward. It was mostly bare there as well, the forest floor littered with leaves and needly plant matting, only further on it thickened.

It was like a very small valley. Hatupatu, creek, other side.

There was almost a rock wall, with one big boulder a little way up the rise on the other side, and he saw a man's head popping up from behind it. Drenched in shadow.

"Give me some help, will you boy?"

He couldn't see the man's head very well; the sunlight didn't penetrate the tree cover higher up. He shuffled forward a few steps, then stopped. He wasn't sure he wanted to go, and his voice carried a hesitancy that belied how scared he was.

"What's the problem?" He asked it too quickly, too nervously. Stammering and shrill. It was very rude to question elders in his tribe. He would get a hard smack for it, if one of them heard, he thought.

"Can you please help me, I'm in pain!" The old man shouted. "I was here picking some herbs for dinner and then a rock rolled onto my leg, *can you help me please?*"

Hatupatu lied to himself about the amount of anger in the man's voice. The man spoke funny, he didn't pronounce very well. Still, only his head was visible.

"Help me *I'm in a lot of pain here!*"

Hatupatu gulped, he wasn't sure what to do. His right hand was unusually sweaty, and his spear felt unnatural and clunky in it. Against his gut instinct he began stepping toward his side of the creek.

He tried holding his spear in a way that looked casual but was ready if he needed to use it.

There were a couple of little stones he could use to step over. He didn't want to get his feet wet as it was a little bit steep on the other side, the creek wasn't very high.

As he neared the creek, the old man's face disappeared behind the rock, and Hatupatu didn't like that. He crossed as quickly as he could, arms in front of him just in case.

There was something unnatural about the man's features. Hatupatu wasn't sure exactly what it was, and when he started up the small rise he looked up once he'd moved onto the area with more leaves on the earth, he could have slipped in the muddier part near the creek.

Still, the man's face was no longer visible. Hatupatu was too low now. He was only about ten metres from the boulder. He didn't want to acknowledge part of his heart jumping like a rabbit in his chest, and he hated the way his voice sounded:

"I'm nearly with you, old man."

He used the formal, generic pronoun. Polite.

The old man stepped out from behind the boulder.

He'd heard a couple of stories about the *moth-men* from the village witch-doctor but never believed. They sounded silly. Impossible.

HORRORific Tales (Cryptids)

It took Hatupatu about two seconds to realize it was a trap. His mind lurched, wishing he'd listened to his intuition and sprinted as soon as he'd heard that awful voice. Into his future it would be forever associated with terror.

In less than a second, the old man's wings billowed out behind him in evil, predatory glory. Iridescent in the droplets of light the forest canopy allowed. Claw fingernails on hands outstretching as his tall body lowered, leaning forward. Husky feet with sharp toenails gripping the mud beneath dead leaves preparing to take off, Hatupatu realized the man was about to fly at him. He wished his spear was already over his shoulder in the throwing position, but it felt heavy and dead. He wanted to raise it but almost second-guessed his intuition and cursed himself for not being quicker.

His arm threw the spear – badly – and it flew past the man's thin, gangly leg into the rise of earth beyond, just shy of the base of a tree. Hatupatu's heart sank, his stomach felt like there was a big rock in it.

He despaired.

How could he fight this awful beast without a weapon?

He couldn't stop looking, the body hair of the man

was so unnatural, so ragged and weird and vulgar, he was so tall and thin, almost a metre taller than the tallest hunter in Hatupatu's village, and not fat or muscular like most men. But his black eyeballs with red hungry pupils expanding were the worst, the crown of his skull appeared to lift and pull his sockets upward, eyes pushed forward with manic thirst. The thin mouth pulling downward didn't look hungry though, it looked malicious and hateful, and as Hatupatu turned around a warm jet of urine erupted from within his flax skirt and trickled down his thigh.

After a couple of bounds he was sprinting, and as he returned to the creek, he'd only passed through less than a minute before, he looked upward to try and figure out a way back. The undergrowth was awfully thick, he would be caged if he couldn't find a way through.

His heart thrashed and his lungs burned in his chest and his legs churned up the dirt more than any race he'd run with the other boys in the village. He heard nothing behind him, the old man must be flying!

HORRORific Tales   (Cryptids)

The village elder had said he'd seen a couple of these awful flying 'moth-men' before, but Hatupatu and the two boys he was with had laughed at the time. Nobody could *fly*. Except it seemed, for this weird man with wings behind his back.

He looked behind, and then he heard it – a wooshing thumping noise as the huge wings thrashed the air just once, and the old man with the crazy face was much, much closer very quickly. An arm holding a dull bone knife led the charge. In half a second Hatupatu had made it across the creek, a few huge steps upward and he leapt into the bush by the Rimu tree he'd come through on the way in.

His only hope was to stay low and let the branches prevent the man's travel toward him… maybe? Strategic thought was starting to leave him, he could feel his mind's need to run, to give in to cowardice, to curl up in a small ball like a baby… he shook his head, he needed his wits about him! His memory conjured up old lessons from the village hunters. Some pig-hunting had been difficult, especially the older, grumpier boars or their wild children… or when a big fat sow had a litter, she was sometimes very protective and fought back. Sometimes the pigs charged, and there were the odd stories of someone being gored, but nothing incredible. Nothing like this.

The mothman crashed into some of the lower, weaker branches and hissed, loud. His wings were mostly useless. Wood cracked and flax was ripped behind Hatupatu who was jumping and running for his life through some of the most tangled undergrowth he'd ever known.

Then something even worse happened – another hideous figure lurched out from behind a tree – a more unnatural and misshapen crone, a female similar to the mothman – sloppy malnourished breasts and a thinner figure lacking all femininity; just vulturish and animalistic, she leapt in a sudden awkward pounce towards Hatupatu who dived to the left, almost falling over onto his face, his arms patted small fronds of trees and he recovered quick, letting out a terrified scream as tears whisked by his eyes.

That just made it difficult to see, and he wiped them away as best he could.

He heard another *whoosh,* no doubt the female was flying after him! Surely the undergrowth was too thick for that?

HORRORific Tales (Cryptids)

Her mouth had opened even further than the first one, and Hatupatu had seen why the man could not pronounce words well – the female's teeth were curved inward like a shark's, all were pointy and shining in the afternoon darkness. She had a small, thin tongue that had wriggled like a malicious, trapped worm.

It would be the ultimate agony to be torn apart, screaming and raw, in their feeding frenzy.

Hatupatu kept sprinting – at least as close to sprinting as he could.

He didn't know the forest perfectly, but he did try and run in the direction of his village – his mind had reached a semblance of balance and sanity, and his self-preservation instinct took over and demanded he go home – after all, there was nowhere else.

… However, it dawned on him that if he did that, he was leading these two awful things *toward* his village… what would happen to the children there, the harmless mums and grandparents?

There were a lot of young children in the village.

Hatupatu swallowed, his heart sinking as he sprinted, and he changed direction to the right. East. He hoped, at least. He'd momentarily lost his bearings. Leaves sparkled in sunlight as he ran through the forest. His heart felt like a volcano about to erupt from his chest.

He could still hear the occasional *woosh* of wing from above, and he looked up as he ran, presumably the female mothman shooting from tree to tree with her enormous wingspan, where the leaves and branches weren't so thick. The male clambering about behind him, but further back.

Relieved, he saw the forest was still thick no matter which way he looked. Not that there was much time spare to glance around. He was confident that there was only forest near him – he'd seen these hills from a distance, and while he hadn't seen the exact area he was in, he'd been higher than this and had not seen clearing.

There was still some hope. It looked to him like he was aimed downhill, and he focused more than he had before… a strength took his mind, and he slowed for a second in temptation, wanting to turn about and face his pursuers. He was so *angry!* How could the old man trick him? How could such wicked things exist?

And if Hatupatu ran back to his village, no doubt there would be warriors and hunters to defend… but there was a lot of grassy area between the forest outskirts and the village, where he would definitely have to fight these two… and without any weapons, without his spear, he would almost definitely lose…

The mothman was still cavorting through the woods behind him, yet further back than before, the sound of breaking small branches and shuffling flax was quieter, but not by much. Hatupatu kept up his speed, cracking his toes against rough roots and tangled fronds. Thankfully his feet were strong with years of hunting, and his youth helped him avoid any traps.

He wondered how far away these awful beings lived from his village… he had only travelled about half a day to get to this part of the woods… but surely the flying people could travel very far, and they must live very far away… surely…?

He wondered how many of them there really were… just one man and woman made sense, but what if there were more…?

Hatupatu thought if he could be silent he could possibly lose the two evil beings that were chasing him. Then he could sneak back to his village. He tried to run quietly, but saw the flickering shadow of the moth-woman flying above.

Her wings were doom, and his heart sank a little.

She could see him from so far above.

He had always been taught by his father that his mind was senior to his body, that of all things he could control, controlling his attitude was most important, and he decided to run even faster – decided that he *could* run even faster, and he chose to run more erratically, trying to zig-zag around in his choice of direction, behind the trees attempting to stay out of sight of the mothwoman's persistent shadow, while not losing speed. He thought of her despicable mouth and shook his head.

It was difficult at first, but then he threw her – he could hear her hissing a little, and the clap of her wings against the air was quieter and further back.

Her mouth was in his mind, old and dirty.

He bounded around the trees, but they were thick and warped and wrong, and it was like they wanted to stop him.

HORRORific Tales   (Cryptids)

He felt like he wanted to hide, but he didn't think he'd made enough distance because he could sometimes hear the two of them communicating. Her, hissing at him, meaning *that village boy is over there! No, to the right! Behind that tree! Keep going!*

Hatupatu almost had a twig in his eye, nearly ran into it, as the mothwoman's filthy maw arose in his memory again and he lost concentration for a moment.

The memory was like he'd opened a coffin, a pit with dead neglected rotting animals in it. Her mouth was the worst thing he'd ever seen in his life.

He ran and ran, part of him wanting to give up. It was downhill, and the forest was a little different, slowly it was changing. A little mistier, hazier. Trees a little shorter. More dead logs he had to be careful of. Most of the time he jumped over them, but sometimes he could only move quickly if he put his weight on them and used them to launch forward.

The mothwoman careened above him, perhaps about ten or twenty metres.

She was laughing a little.

She knew he would be out of breath soon, and Hatupatu knew that she knew.

No doubt, he would probably die.

Still, at least his village would be safe. For now.

He was crying, and he knew he couldn't afford the luxury. He wanted again, felt the temptation to give into his darkest emotions, to give up, to yield to this evil, to let them take him and eat him – it would only be a small time, a few seconds of pain, then what -? Nothing? Nothing forever?

Was there an afterlife, a world beyond this? Were the strange visions of the village witch-doctor true, or made up? They must be true, after all the *mothmen* were true, they were real.

And they *ate people.* They were *cannibals*… and they *flew*… no doubt they tore shreds off people like Hatupatu and flayed skin with their angry claws and elated when they squeezed the blood from dripping human meat…

He couldn't hear any crashing behind him, and a second of relief beckoned him to slow down, but he realized why as a second shadow glided into the first.

HORRORific Tales (Cryptids)

They didn't need to chase through the undergrowth. They would just wait until he became too tired to run. Then eat him when he was exhausted. It was a simple tactic for catching large, or unruly animals. A sob escaped his mouth.

He looked around so fast for a long branch he could use as a weapon, but there was nothing, and no time to grab it. And if he did manage to rip off one of these tree branches as he sprinted by, so what? It wouldn't be much good, except for a bludgeoning weapon.

The pig-spears he and the hunters from his village used were sharpened, weighted, perfectly balanced, wood selected after many days journey and comparison in different parts of the forest, then taken to the village shrine for blessing and painting. Nothing was done in an instant.

Hatupatu cried as he ran, sobbing, tears like a powerful creek down his cheeks. At least he'd led these two away from his village, down a hill somewhere. He didn't know where and *wished* he hadn't come all this way by himself. He should have asked someone else to come with him, but his adventurous spirit had taken over, and he'd left so early few others in the village had been awake.

Their shadows moved far away, it meant there must be a lot of tree cover, a lot of low, abundant branches.

He looked up, slowing down a little.

If he was to fight them, now was the time to grab something to use as a weapon… a branch… an old dead bit of wood… even a flying man couldn't handle a huge club to the head.

Maybe he could even defeat them!

He noticed a dark, strong-looking piece of wood poking up out of a clump of lush moss. It looked dead and mostly rotting, but he pulled, still jogging, and it came free. It was about the width of his fist, and he squeezed it.

Tight. It withstood his grasp, and he smiled a little as he ran, trying to pick up the pace without falling or stumbling. He couldn't afford to be distracted by a lump of wood, even one that may possibly save his life.

He swung his makeshift club as he ran.

There was hope!

HORRORific Tales   (Cryptids)

He heard a screeching from above that was unlike the other two, and a shadow like the others flew over him. But it came from in front of him, like the screeching noise. Blobs of moss and wood were falling off his makeshift club, and he thought he should test the other end.

As he was about to feel it, a good chunk of it flaked away, it was filled with slaters. The wood was old and eaten away. His club was barely as long as his forearm. It had distracted him, and he threw the rest of it away, it wouldn't be much use.

He kept running, swiping bugs off his arm. He looked up, and it was darker here in this part of the forest.

And then he was stepping on wood. On wooden stairs, almost. Some kind of ramp. Wooden branches scraped a little to make a kind of path. Around him, high up in the trees, were huts. Dozens of mothmen circled above.

He'd ran into their camp…

Still, at least he'd kept them away from his village! He was happy about that.

He wondered if they'd take him prisoner or just eat him.

There were no obvious bloodstains around, perhaps they dined in a vaguely communal or gentle fashion.

Screeching filled his ears.

He'd done the right thing, he'd led them away from his family, his friends and others. All he could do now was a momentary prayer, then put up the best fight he could.

A mothman ran out of a tree hut, probably because of the screeching. His mouth dripped blood, and he was eating something dark with a red stain on it. Hatupatu looked all around, raising his arms, he wanted to at least get a few shots in before they killed him. In the corner of his eye, a corpse fell from the sky, thudding on the ground. In one of the other trees, a couple of mothmen hunched over a body with still legs, their heads bobbing up and down. They were eating it.

The mothman who came out of the tree hut threw his dinner at Hatupatu… it was a head! It struck his thigh and fell by his foot as the mothman leaned forward, wings billowing out to engulf his world.

HORRORific Tales   (Cryptids)

Hatupatu's despair overwhelmed him, and he sank to his knees.

He didn't want to be near the head, and stepped back without thinking, until he recognized the earrings, the tattoos. Falling, he turned the head over in his tender hands and took one final look at his mother.

The screeching became louder, joyous. Celebrating. *Hungry…*

But Hatupatu found peace. He just looked into that woman's eyes, ignoring the hole in her head where half the sausages of her brain gristle had been chewed and slopped out, ignoring the trip-trap of mothman clawed toes clacking against the wooden makeshift path louder and louder towards him, ignoring the shadow of many wings darkening his last day, and felt all the love he could, felt the rightness of him being with her, as they descended upon him.

Check out Arthur's work here:

The Devil's Fingertips

by
Gary Batchelor

HORRORific Tales   (Cryptids)

> All down the church in the midst of fire,
>
> The hellish monster flew,
>
> And passing onward to the quire,
>
> He many people slew
>
> Unknown

'This black dog, or the divel in such a linenesse (God hee knoweth al who worketh all,) running all along down the body of the church with great swiftnesse, and incredible haste, among the people, in a visible fourm and shape, passed between two persons, as they were kneeling uppon their knees, and occupied in prayer as it seemed, wrung the necks of them bothe at one instant clene backward, in somuch that even at a moment where they kneeled, they strangely dyed.'

Rev Abraham Fleming,

'A Straunge and Terrible Wunder'

1577

St Mary's Church

Bungay

Suffolk

August 4th 1577

The congregation had assembled for worship, despite the intensity of the violent storm that continued to rage outside its hallowed walls.

Mutterings could be heard, commenting on the ferocity of the terrible and fearful tempest, as the winds blew, making the building shudder, as though through fear. The interior was plunged into almost darkness, save the meagre light from the candles, some of which had blown out. The rain and hail lashed down in a biblical deluge, as flashes of forked and ribbon lightning illuminated the interior. These strikes were swiftly followed by massive crashes of thunder, clearly overhead, that shook the church to its very foundations.

HORRORific Tales   (Cryptids)

At that precise moment, the massive oak doors to the church burst open and an enormous black dog, larger than a pony, came hurtling amok along the body of the church, at incredible speed. It rushed about in a fury as though it only had limited time as another burst of lightning struck close to the open doors of the church.

Although some parishioners were standing, some were still kneeling as they prayed for mercy. It was one of those, a man, that the beast launched itself at, grabbing hold of his throat in its salivating, terrible jaws. It brutally shook its head from side to side, tearing into the tissue and causing a strangulated scream to begin, but never finished.

The blood cascaded from the wound, showering other parishioners in a slick, red veil.

Dropping the cadaver the beast leapt towards another man and struck his back, pushing him face down into the floor. The jaws of the fiend latched onto the back of the neck and crushed through skin, bone and tissue. Blood spouted like a geyser into the air and those close to the cascade tried, with mixed fortunes, to evade the splatter.

The creature, its eyes gleaming red with fire, almost casually looked around the congregation.

Some were praying on their knees to be delivered from this hellhound, others were moving towards the door, despite the howling gale and lashing rain that continued to batter the building.

This harbinger of death and destruction then took off again, leaping at one, then two, then three people in quick succession as it made its way towards the exit.

These three people were fortunate, in that they only received lacerations from the beast's claws.

The worshippers watched in stunned amazement and fear as this Cerberus shot through the church's doors and disappeared from their sight.

It would be much later, when their horror at what had occurred had calmed, that it was commented that at no point did the footfalls of the hound's paws make any noticeable sound.

From a distance a mourning howl was heard, that made the blood run cold of all who heard it.

Thirteen miles to the southeast lay the village of Blythburgh.

The storm continued unabated, if anything, increasing in its savagery.

But in Holy Trinity Church at Blythburgh the congregation were blissfully unaware of the bloodshed that had taken place at Bungay.

The sermon that day had concerned the Devil and all his works, and as if to lend reality to those words, a shuddering clap of thunder shattered the air causing the building to quake and groan. Many interpreted the storm as a sign of God's displeasure at their sinning ways.

The doors to the church flew open and the monstrous, snarling black apparition crashed in, running through the congregation, people trying to avoid the fiend, upsetting benches and littering the pews with carnage.

An elderly man, too old and infirm to move quick enough was grabbed and shaken like a rat before being discarded like a used toy. No one moved to help him, they were too concerned with their own welfare and so he slowly bled to death. Then a boy, who had stayed close to his parents, suddenly made a dash for the open doorway, but was run down and brutally eviscerated.

Appearing to be content with its predation, the beast left the remains of the boy and made towards the door.

The rain, hail, thunder and lightning had been relentless, but the creature paused on the threshold of the church, before a shard of lightning hit the steps of the church at the precise moment that the hellhound dragged its claws across the church door in an apparent symbolic sign of what? Possession? Damnation? A warning?

The combination of claw and lightning left scorch marks on the church door that would endure and become known as the Devil's fingerprints.

As would the terror and revulsion that was wrought that day in both Bungay and Blythburgh.

Dr Leah Dutton sat back in her chair and cast her eyes over the screen.

The first draft of many, no doubt.

She had made notes from her research online and then typed up an overall account from the two sixteenth century church reports in her own words.

The myth of Black Shuck was a recent interest and had stemmed, in part from her research and papers about The Beast of Bodmin, as well as other canine and feline tales and folklore.

HORRORific Tales (Cryptids)

One of the difficulties she was experiencing was that the Bodmin Moor feline was of recent origin, with pictures, oral evidence and many sightings from the 1980's onwards, while the Black Shuck was far more mythological and therefore, more difficult to pin down.

She had visited both church's and seen the scorch marks on the church door for herself.

But were they caused by a massive canine, with fiery eyes and glowing claws? Or could it have been because of the storm on that day, almost four hundred and fifty years ago?

There had been sightings of Black Shuck more recently in 1901 as well as the 1970's and 1980's, which she would also document.

The first ever mention of this fenland apparition occurred in 1127, where the word 'shuck' the Old English for devil, 'succa' first appeared. It was all to do with religion apparently and the arrival of Henry of Poitou as the new abbot of Peterborough Abbey, set the wheels in motion for the appearance of mysterious huntsman, the so called 'Wild Hunt,' riding their mounts accompanied by their black hounds baying for blood from the start of Lent until Easter.

But the real reason she had begun to investigate the Black Schuck was because of a recent spate of attacks on livestock, mainly sheep, but also several cows in an area associated with the demon.

Leah had already travelled to three of the sites and talked with the farmers and as many local people as she could find.

The consensus was that the attacks were just ordinary dogs, off the lead, who couldn't be controlled by their owners and ran amok.

She had also tried to liaise with the local constabulary, there were those officers who had responsibility for rural affairs, after all. But she had been given scant attention, and her queries had been dismissed, almost as interfering.

Leah just wanted to get to the truth of these attacks, nothing more.

The three attacks she had investigated had occurred in an area south of Norwich and north of the A143.

HORRORific Tales (Cryptids)

Over the Easter holiday she had rented a holiday cottage for a week in Halesworth and spent a week walking the area, talking to any local she came across and quizzing them about the recent attacks, but also the myth of Black Shuck.

The responses to her questions were many and varied. Some stated they were too busy to bother with such nonsense, while others were prepared to talk about the attacks, and had an opinion on the demon dog.

For the most part, the consensus was that the attacks were caused by poorly trained dogs, off the lead, owned by poorly trained owners.

But one or two, older people it had to be said, were prepared to admit that these attacks were suspicious because of the number of them in a very short space of time.

There had been three in a week, and overall, around seven in a seven-month period.

One elderly farmer, Frank Howard, was particularly keen to talk to Leah as he had discovered five lambs dead and partially eaten the very morning she passed by his farm.

He offered to take her to the field where they were killed as well as the carcasses themselves.

When she asked his opinion on what had killed the lambs, his response was unequivocal.

'I'm of the generation that remembers the myths and folklore of the hellhound, Black Shuck, as told to me by my parents, and there's before them.

I admit it's easier to just blame some mythical beast for acts that a domestic dog might perpetrate, but through the hundreds of years that this land has been farmed, there have been far too many attacks to be attributed to dogs off the lead. I countenance that there is an argument for a pack of feral dogs roaming the countryside, but there's no sightings, nor any evidence for that.'

When she asked Frank about why the attacks in the 16th century had been on parishioners in two church's his response was terse.

'All to do with the two faiths, Protestant and Catholic I reckon. I don't know why a demon dog was brought to life, but it was and there you are. Sounds to me there was people not happy about the way the church was going. Not that I'm a religious man, but they were in those times.'

I asked what he meant by that.

'Are you suggesting that one of those faiths somehow bought the hellhound to life in an attempt to destroy the other?'

He fixed me with his calm yet determined grey eyes. 'I'm not saying how they did it, mighten be a possibility though, wouldn't you say?'

This was not a theory Leah had come across before and it intrigued her.

Her thoughts turned to the quote by the Reverend Fleming in his treatise, A Strange and Terrible Wonder written at the time of the two attacks in the churches, when he said, '*this black dog or the devil in such a likeness.*'

Were the two branches of the church so estranged from each other that they would wish to bring about the annihilation of the other and would inveigle the manifestation of the devil as a weapon in the form of a hellhound?

That's a bit naive, isn't it? The animosity was there for all to see during the various struggles for dominance throughout the ages. The obliteration of one or the other would have led to a clear, solitary path.

The seven days passed by in a blur as she so enjoyed walking, especially when it didn't tend to involve many hills.

Leah recollected that there had been some sightings and stories from on or around the coast of Suffolk, and she determined that on the next break she would endeavour to take a similar fact-obtaining exercise.

The next break was the summer holidays, and she took herself off to the Suffolk coast for a week in August. It was the height of the school holidays, but she reasoned that she would be so absorbed in her quest and would therefore barely register the myriad of kids.

Rather than stay in one place and return every night, on this occasion she decided to stay at a different place every night. She planned out her itinerary and started north of Felixstowe, at Bawdsey.

She didn't rush and spent as much time talking to the locals as she could find. Some were more willing to converse with her than others, but after the first day she wondered whether she was going to discover much at all.

No one appeared to have knowledge or interest in Black Shuck and despite the apparent recording of the beast's presence in the vicinity, no one she approached appeared to know much about it at all.

Over the next few days she passed through Aldeburgh and Thorpeness, then skirted around Sizewell B Power Station before taking some timeout with a visit to Minsmere, the RSPB reserve. She needed a break from demon entities and religious battles on a supernatural front.

Not that she knew much about birds, although after visiting the reserve she found that her interest had been kindled, and she may well do more of it in the future.

North of the power station was the village of Dunwich. She knew this name from a story written by H P Lovecraft, called The Dunwich Horror, although the Dunwich he referred to was a fictional place set in Massachusetts.

She knew this because her mother had been a Reader in American Literature and had written numerous papers on Lovecraft, who was a strange man with views that would have been at odds with today's society.

The Dunwich Horror, which she had read many years earlier featured a peculiar family called the Whateleys. This was a pivotal novella in Lovecraft's Cthulhu Mythos and featured such staples as the Miskatonic University and the Necronomicon.

The village on the coast of Suffolk was mentioned in the Domesday Book of 1086 in which it had three churches and an estimated population of 3000. Considerably more than the numbers who live there today.

In Saxon times it was known to have been a significant port.

Leah next stayed in Walberswick, a village that had many second homes and so was largely deserted in winter.

That was not the first time she had encountered that phenomenon.

As she approached her final day, she was alerted to a recently broken story about a man having been attacked by some type of creature on a farm close to the village of Chillesford. It was in a relatively sparsely populated area, which comprised farmland together with some landscape sites and Tunstall Forest.

HORRORific Tales   (Cryptids)

She decided she was too close to miss this opportunity and left immediately to see what she could discover.

Very little was the answer.

The farmer had died, and although there were suspicious circumstances, there was nothing to indicate whether it had been an accident or something more sinister. The involvement of some animal had apparently been someone with a vivid imagination.

She spent some time trying to glean any snippets, and details of the farmer and what might be afoot.

But Leah eventually grew weary of going around in circles and decided to take a leisurely drive home.

She made for the Orford Road, the B1078, intending to turn left towards Tunstall, rather than turn round and use the B1084 to Woodbridge.

She came up to the junction, suddenly realising how tired she felt.

Returning home was the sensible option.

She pulled onto the road to Tunstall intending to pass through it on her way to picking up the A12.

Reassured now she was on her way back to familiar surroundings she thought about the week and what new details had emerged.

She was pleased she had come to the area. There was nothing that came close to being at the scene, or close to it of an incident, to make you feel your part of it.

That had certainly been the case when she had traced her fingertips over the scorch marks on the church door. She felt transported back to that time, and she wondered what she would have made of what had occurred.

She was driving leisurely along the B road, her full beam prominent so she could see clearly in front of her.

The road wasn't narrow by any means, but neither was it an A road. Some of the edges were uneven and she didn't want to inadvertently hit the road edge.

Her beam illuminated the woodland on either side of the road and her eyes kept being distracted by what she thought was movement, a shadow passing between the upright sentinels of trees.

She was distracted by these apparent apparitions, as well as in assessing what she had learned, when in her rearview mirror she saw two pinpricks of a pale red light.

She returned her eyes to the road in front of her and thought nothing more of it.

Except, that when she glanced in the mirror moments later the two pinpricks had grown considerably bigger, and the light red colour was now unmistakeably crimson.

Are those lights even legal?

That they were getting closer, at speed was clear.

Whatever.

She continued her focus on the road ahead of her, but her eyes were now repeatedly drawn to the approaching vehicle in her rear-view mirror.

She smiled. *Maybe it's Black Shuck come to give me a send-off.*

The smile froze on her face as the two red orbs, now blindingly close did indeed resemble the two red eyes attributed to the demon and were now less than fifty metres from her bumper.

He's driving like a maniac.

In a split second the car was on her bumper and then past her, barely a coat of paint between them.

Leah was gripping onto the steering wheel, but even so the blur that was the other vehicle caused her hands to slip, and before she knew it, she caught the edge of the road and lost control.

Her last thought before she bounced off the road, onto the vegetation and then hit the tree, as the airbag filled the space between her and the dashboard, was that she should have pulled over into one of the passing places.

***

Leah groaned and could feel liquid trickling somewhere but felt too out of it to be sure where.

Slowly her eyes opened. There wasn't much difference between having her eyes open or closed. Everything was black.

She blinked a few times, as much to allow herself time for her head to clear, as much as anything else.

Don't move too soon. Allow yourself time to adjust.

She had no idea how long she had been unconscious.

She took a few breaths, careful, controlled and felt a little better. It also confirmed she hadn't damaged her torso, at least not so it impacted her breathing.

The airbag had deflated a little and so after deciding she had remained passive long enough, she first moved one arm, then the other.

So far so good.

Then she performed a similar process with her legs, although her pelvis complained a bit as she moved her right leg.

Right, now for the ultimate test.

She stretched across her body with her left arm, as she simultaneously twisted her body to the right, feeling for the seat belt release below.

The exertion wasn't painful, but it still took some effort before she found the button, pressed it and the belt released its hold.

She allowed herself a moment to recover.

Leah searched the door for the handle with her right hand, found it and the door opened, making grinding protest noises as it did so.

Leah pushed the door fully open, and a strong breeze caught it and made it shudder in her hand.,

The wind's picked up.

Slowly, not wishing to make a potentially bad situation worse, she cautiously swung her right leg out of the vehicle, twisting as she did so. She then allowed her left leg to catch up and planted both feet firmly on the ground. She was shaking.

Although she had managed to move, she still felt several pains in her back and side as she did so.

I'll ignore them. More pressing issues to deal with now.

All lights on the vehicle were either smashed or not working, so her world remained in darkness.

I need a light.

She cautiously began to stand, her legs shaking, not with the effort but the traumatic nature of her situation.

She wasn't scared of the dark or anything like that, at least, she didn't think she was, but this was a strange set of circumstances she found herself in.

Alone in the dark? How do you know?

Why that thought intruded into her consciousness at precisely that moment she couldn't have said, but it did further unsettle her.

Leah allowed her eyes to accommodate to the darkness, before she felt her way around the back of the car, moving cautiously over the uneven vegetation, until she came to the passenger door.

Feeling for the handle, she depressed it and pulled. Like the driver's side, the door groaned in protest at being opened, the impact with the tree having misaligned the wing, pushing it up into the door frame.

But it opened.

Using her hands she felt on the seat for her bag, but it was empty. She continued exploring the interior and found it in the car well. Leah opened it and searched the interior for her mobile.

Got it.

She brought it out and unlocked it with her fingerprint.

It activated at once, causing Leah to sigh with relief. To her surprise the time was 10.15 pm. She sighed.

Only for the sigh to catch in her throat as she heard a low moaning coming from somewhere around her.

Was that the breeze? Two branches rubbing together?

Switching the light on she held it up and began to explore her immediate surroundings. The light was poor, limited in its luminescence, but it didn't reveal anything she was concerned about. But that didn't slow down her accelerated heartbeat one iota

Her eye caught the front of the car and the tree she'd hit.

That won't be usable in a hurry.

She was going to have to walk back to civilisation.

Leah retrieved her bag from the car well, closed the passenger door and angled her phone so the light illuminated the boot. On opening it, she removed her rucksack containing her clothes and toiletries and shut it with a loud thump. It seemed to echo around her. She shook her head and used the light to show her where the road edge was.

It was then that she thought, for the first time, about the behaviour of the motorist who had forced her off the road.

This wasn't her fault. But there was little point in getting angry or frustrated at her predicament.

It's happened and I just must deal with it.

Leah shone the light over the car, for one final look.

She grimaced. *Annoying.*

She loaded the rucksack on her back and began walking along the edge of the road towards Tunstall.

She had covered no more than twenty-five paces before she froze. She thought she heard a deep rumbling growl from somewhere in the forest.

She gritted her teeth. *Pull yourself together, you're a bag of nerves.*

She began walking again, trying to work out how far she was from Tunstall and so how long it might take her.

She could have got the map from her bag but didn't think it was worth stopping to do that. She had looked at the map often enough to have a rough idea and thought that maybe she had two and a half, maybe three miles to walk. Not too far under normal circumstances, but these weren't normal by any means.

That said, she was grateful that she wasn't injured, so that was a blessing.

Leah managed to get into a rhythm and her stride length began to increase as her thoughts turned to what she would do when she reached Tunstall.

She thought there were two pubs in the village, The Tunstall Green Man in the centre, while the Plough and Sail lay just outside. She hoped at least one of them would be opened by the time she reached there.

HORRORific Tales (Cryptids)

An owl hooting made her jump, and she smiled ruefully to herself at her unease.

She was just beginning to relax when suddenly the light on her phone cut out.

Oh fuck.

She inspected the device, fiddling with it in a vain attempt to reactivate it, but it steadfastly refused to cooperate.

Oh well.

She moved closer to where she thought the middle of the road was and slowed her pace. She didn't want to trip on the edge of the road and take a tumble.

There wasn't a moon, so could expect no help from that orb, so continued her trek, suddenly feeling hungry. She hadn't eaten since this morning.

The owl hooted again, but this time she didn't react.

Just to make sure though, she stopped, turned and looked behind her.

Unsurprisingly she couldn't see anything. *Now your just being silly.*

The whining growl had reached a crescendo before it gradually faded away, leaving her by the roadside unsure of her situation, surroundings or sanity.

All I need to do is sleep. Is that a dog howling somewhere in the distance?

I don't care, I just want to close my eyes, then all will be well. All will be well.

Her final thought as she drifted into unconsciousness once again, was that even if Black Shuck was stalking her, she wouldn't be able to hear his approach because his paws didn't make a sound. It was like it was walking on air.

Check out Gary's work here:

HORRORific Tales   (Cryptids)

Thank you for taking the time to enjoy these stories. Please be sure to follow our authors by using the QR codes and pick up their work. Until next time our friends. Remember to keep it creepy, keep it HORRORific!

The Cryptid Catalogue

Taniwha

In Māori mythology, a "taniwha" refers to a supernatural creature, often depicted as a water spirit, monster, or powerful being, that can take various forms like eels, sharks, or whales, and is believed to live in deep pools, rivers, caves, or the sea

Jersey Devil

The "Jersey Devil" is said to roam the New Jersey Pinelands and many people have told others of scary encounters on dark nights in the wilderness of the Pines. Its screams are said to be quite chilling to the spine.The creature is believed to be the unwanted thirteenth child of Mother Leeds.

HORRORific Tales   (Cryptids)

Bigfoot

Bigfoot, also known as Sasquatch, is a legendary, large, hairy, human-like creature said to inhabit forests, particularly in the Pacific Northwest of North America.

Werewolf

The Werewolf, also known as a Lycanthrope Wolfman or Dogman, is a mythological or folkloric human with the ability to shape shift into a wolf or an anthropomorphic wolf-like creature, either purposely or after being placed under a curse.

Giant Arachnids

The J'ba FoFi, also known as the Congolese Giant Spiders, are a type of large arachnid cryptid which is said to inhabit the forests of the Congo, possibly representing a new species of Arachnida.

The Witch Owl

La Lechuza, the Witch Owl, is said to be a witch that can shapeshift into an owl and is well-known throughout Mexico and Texas.

HORRORific Tales   (Cryptids)

Cherufe

In Mapuche mythology, a "Cherufe" is a mythical, man-eating creature made of rock crystals and magma, said to inhabit volcanic regions and be responsible for earthquakes and volcanic eruptions.

Gruagach

The Gruagach, also known as the Grogoch, Gelt, or on occasion, the Puka is a large, bipedal ape-like creature that allegedly lives in Ireland. The creature appears in mythology around Ireland and is sighted only on rare occasions.

Lyngbakr

The Lyngbakr is the name of a massive whale-like sea monster reported in the Örvar-Odds saga to have existed in the Greenland Sea. According to the saga, Lyngbakr would bait seafarers by posing as a heather-covered island, and when a crew landed on his back, he sank into the sea, drowning the crew.

Mothman

The Mothman is a cryptid, or mythical creature, that originated in Point Pleasant, West Virginia, in the late 1960s, described as a large, winged, humanoid figure with glowing red eyes, often associated with impending disasters

HORRORific Tales (Cryptids)

Black Shuck

The Black Shuck, Old Shuck, Old Shock or simply Shuck is the name given to a ghostly black dog which is said to roam the coastline and countryside of East Anglia.

Also Available

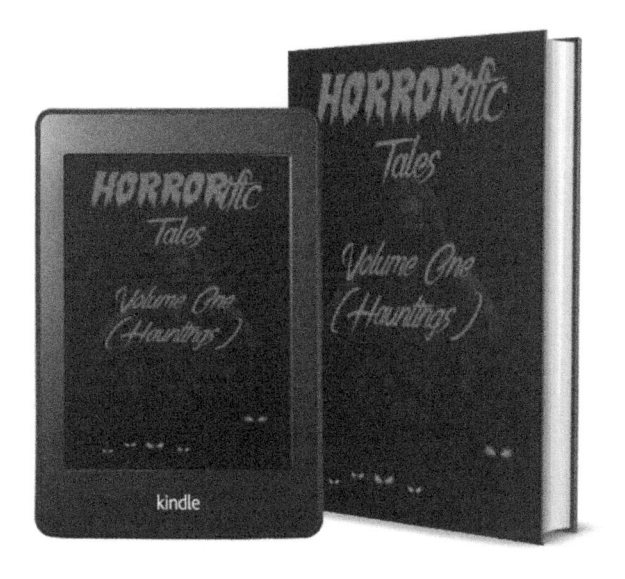

Printed and bound by CPI Group (UK) Ltd, Croydon, CR0 4YY
01/04/2025
01839455-0001